THE SNOWMAN CODE

THE SNOWMAN CODE

SIMON STEPHENSON

Illustrated by Reggie Brown

First published in the United Kingdom by
HarperCollins *Children's Books* in 2024
HarperCollins *Children's Books* is a division of HarperCollins*Publishers* Ltd
1 London Bridge Street
London SE1 9GF

www.harpercollins.co.uk

HarperCollins*Publishers*
Macken House, 39/40 Mayor Street Upper
Dublin 1, D01 C9W8, Ireland

1

ISBN 978–0–00–866876–1

Simon Stephenson and Reggie Brown assert the moral right to be identified as the author and illustrator of the work respectively.
A CIP catalogue record for this title is available from the British Library.

Typeset in Aldus LT Std 11/18pt
Printed and bound in the UK using 100% renewable electricity at
CPI Group (UK) Ltd

For snowmen everywhere

A NOTE TO YOUNGER READERS:

This story is best read when it feels like winter.

That doesn't mean you can only read it when there is snow outside. After all, it doesn't only ever feel like winter because there is snow outside. Sometimes it can feel like winter because there is snow inside.

I hope that if you read this story at such a time, it might warm you. Just the same way it warmed me when I first heard it from some of the people it actually happened to.

A NOTE TO OLDER READERS:

All the above goes for you too.

One

It was the longest winter there had been in over three hundred years.

It had happened because the weather was broken now.

At least, everybody kept saying that was why it had happened.

Even the kids in the school playground said so.

Imagine that: kids with nothing better to talk about than the weather!

Not that Blessing was ever at school to hear the other kids talk about the weather.

She had not been to school since December.

And now it was March.

The reason Blessing had stopped going to school was because she had a problem. In fact, she had three problems, and they were all in her class: Ashby Tregdahornick, Cynthia Smith-Smith and Bartholomew Weaselton.

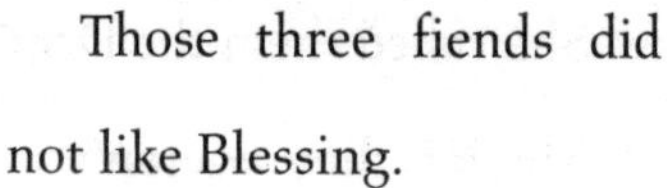

Those three fiends did not like Blessing.

She did not know why.

Maybe it was because Blessing was always polite and kind.

Or because she was good at art and maths and science.

Or because she could

speak French like a Parisian, whereas when any of those three tried, they sounded like a pack of stray dogs gargling with cough mixture.

Whatever their reason, they did mean things to her.

They hid her uniform after swimming.

They tore up her projects.

They even called her ridiculous names that did not make any sense!

Blessing had her own name for them, and it certainly did make sense.

She called them the Driplet Triplets.

Maybe they weren't real triplets, but there were three of them, and they were always together. And what is a bully if not a drip? And if a bully is a drip then a young bully must surely be a driplet. It was mean to call people names, so Blessing had never actually called them the Driplet Triplets out loud. Still, as far as she knew, there was no rule against thinking it.

If it had been any other season, Blessing would have

told her mum, and the Driplet Triplets would have been in big trouble. They might have even been put into different classes. And if that happened they would probably all have immediately died.

But it was still winter. And Blessing couldn't possibly tell her mum about bullies in winter.

It would make her mum sad, and Margaret was quite sad enough already.

Margaret was already so sad that sometimes she did not even go to work any more.

If she got any sadder, Blessing might be sent away again.

Blessing had been sent away twice before.

Both times had been in winter, and both had been because Margaret had become very sad.

What happened was that Jasmine came to the door and pretended it was just a normal visit. But soon enough an ambulance arrived for Margaret and took her away.

And then Jasmine took Blessing to Miriam and John's house.

And left her there.

It was not Margaret's fault that winter made her so sad. After all, when she was a little girl, Margaret had lived in a country where there was no such thing as winter. Yet here in London she was expected to spend several months of every year freezing cold!

It was a bit much.

If you asked her, Margaret would tell you that the reason she disliked winter was not because it was so cold, or so dark, or even because the whole thing was such a ridiculous idea. She would tell you it was because winter made all the beautiful roses in the Rose Garden in Victoria Park disappear.

And what could possibly be the point of a season that did that?

Not even Dr Kumar had been able to answer that.

Instead, he had prescribed Margaret a special lamp. He had said it was so much like the sun that it would make her feel very happy indeed.

The day it arrived had been like Christmas. Blessing had torn open the box, and then Margaret had plugged the lamp in. They had both stared at it, then told each other that it was indeed just exactly like the sun.

But then Blessing had asked Margaret if she felt happier. Margaret had said she didn't just yet, but she was sure she would by the next morning. After all, the lamp was just like the sun!

But Margaret was not any happier by the next morning.

If anything, she was just a little sadder.

Because the lamp was not really anything like the sun.

After all, it was just a lamp.

And the sun is the sun.

Anyway, that is why Blessing had not been to school since December.

Because Dr Kumar's lamp had not worked.

And the Driplet Triplets were awful.

And she couldn't tell her mum about them in winter.

Because she did not want Jasmine to come and send her away again.

Of course, not going to school was itself exactly the kind of thing that could get you sent away.

Luckily, Blessing was an expert at doing her mum's handwriting, so she had written a note to Miss Hazelworst. It explained that Blessing and Margaret were moving to the outback of Australia to run a kangaroo sanctuary, and nobody would ever hear from them again.

Miss Hazelworst had cried and told Blessing she was the best Year Five student she'd ever had.

Blessing had told Miss Hazelworst the nicest true thing

that she could, which was that Miss Hazelworst was the very best Year Five teacher she'd ever had.

Every morning since then, Blessing had got dressed in her uniform, brushed her teeth, kissed her mum goodbye and set off through Victoria Park as if she was going to school. Then, each afternoon, she came home and told her mum about the things that had happened at school that day. Of course, Blessing had to make all those things up, but Margaret was too sad to notice.

The only real problem with not going to school was that Blessing still had to go somewhere. And not just any old somewhere, but somewhere you could go if you were ten-and-a-half years old, were wearing your school uniform and had only your lunch money to spend.

Sometimes Blessing went to the big museum with the giant stuffed walrus and tagged on to other kids' class trips. If anyone asked her what she was doing, she pretended to be an exchange student from France. Afterwards, she went to Leicester Square and hid herself amidst coach parties of

old people as they entered their matinees at the theatre.

Once, when she was very bored indeed, Blessing even went to the children's hospital and pretended to be a patient. She had to run away when a nurse tried to put her arm in plaster.

On other days, Blessing went to a cinema she had found, where a window in the toilets was always left open. It was only a small window, but it was just the right size that a ten-and-a-half-year-old girl could squeeze through it, so long as it was before lunch. It was warm inside the cinema, and people often left behind nearly full buckets of popcorn that Blessing could eat for lunch. If she watched the movie three or four times, Blessing could easily pass a whole day there.

As long as she remembered to stay out later on Tuesdays, Blessing's system worked very well. Blessing was supposed to go to after-school Art Club on Tuesday, and she loved it so much that even Margaret might notice if she came home too early that day.

Of course, Tuesday also happens to be the day of the week that things most like to change on. Monday is just a little too early in the week for things to change, but Wednesday is a little too late. Tuesday is the perfect day for things to change on, and somehow things seem to know that, and always do their very best to change on a Tuesday.

Sure enough, it was on a Tuesday – a Tuesday when Blessing had even remembered to stay out later – that everything changed forever.

Two

It was still too early for Blessing to go home when she got off the bus that Tuesday, so she decided to take a detour through Victoria Park.

She checked nobody was watching, then climbed the gate.

Crunch!

Blessing landed in the snow on the other side of the gate. There was still snow everywhere in the city, of course,

but here in the park it was deeper. And, with the moon now shining on it, it even seemed to glow a little.

(Perhaps you are wondering what time it was, if it was already dark and the moon was shining? Well, it was only just gone half past four! Because, even though it was now March, it was still the depths of winter. The people on television said this was yet another sign that the weather really was broken.)

As Blessing crossed the park, she could hear her feet crunching in the snow.

Crunch-slurp-crunch-slurp-crunch-slurp.

The crunch was her boots pressing down in the snow. The slurp was the snow trying to steal them as she lifted them back up. Experienced Norwegians will tell you that snow only gets that boot-stealing way when it has been on the ground for a long time. This snow had been here since November. People had begun to complain that they could not even remember what the ground looked like.

Crunch-slurp-crunch-slurp-crunch-slurp.

As Blessing made her way across the bridge that ran over the frozen pond, the ducks quacked loudly at her.

'I know, ducks,' Blessing told them. 'We just have to wait until spring.'

The largest duck quacked back angrily.

'Well, so everybody keeps saying,' Blessing said. 'But complaining about it won't make spring come any quicker, you know.'

Blessing continued on, across the pitches.

On a normal Tuesday afternoon in late spring, there'd be evening sunlight.

There'd be kids playing just as far as the eye could see.

There'd be dogs chasing tennis balls.

And old people doing tai chi.

And mixed in with all the yelling and the barking, and the strange creaking noises that old people make when

they do tai chi, there would be the hissing of the sprinklers that would keep the grass on the pitches bright green until midsummer.

On this Tuesday afternoon, though, there was only moonlit snow and darkness and silence.

And also a quite unfortunate-looking snowman.

Some kids had built him back when the snow first fell.

They had done a terrible job.

For one thing, he was lopsided.

For another, they hadn't had any carrots or coal or any of the other things that a snowman is supposed to be made from.

So his eyes were made of bottle-tops.

His eyebrows were twigs.

His nose was a small old potato.

His mouth had been drawn on with a finger.

The hair on the top of his head was a few fallen leaves.

And a muddy and threadbare old scarf hung around his neck.

If somebody had drawn such a snowman at Art Club, Blessing would have given that kid a 3/10, and everybody knew she was one of the most generous graders around.

At the far edge of the pitches, Blessing reached the playground and climbed on to one of the swings. Expertly moving her legs in time, she swung higher and higher until she could see beyond the Rose Garden and out of the park, and even across to her own street. And if she turned her head the other way, she could see the pitches, and the duck pond, and the bus stop, and beyond that the lights of the city itself and—

And right then, that was when she saw it.

The snowman.

The 3/10, lopsided snowman.

The one with bottle-tops for eyes, twigs for eyebrows, a

potato for a nose, a drawn-on mouth, leaves for hair and a muddy and threadbare old scarf.

The snowman that was, well, moving.

He stood up straight, stretched his arms, yawned and looked around the park.

And that was when he saw Blessing on her swing.

For a moment their eyes met.

Hers, brown and astonished.

His, bottle-tops and horrified.

The snowman froze.

And then he slowly lowered his arms and slouched back down to his lopsided position, until he looked just like an ordinary 3/10 snowman again.

Blessing stopped moving her legs.

Her swing squeaked to a standstill.

Had that really just happened?

Well, yes.

It had just happened.

Blessing had seen it happen.

Blessing climbed down from the swing and walked back across the pitches until she was face to face with the snowman.

'Excuse me?' she said. 'Hello?'

The snowman did not reply, but stared straight ahead.

'Can you hear me?' asked Blessing.

The snowman only continued to stare straight ahead.

'Excuse me!' Blessing said again. 'I asked you if you can hear me?'

The snowman remained still, but Blessing could see his breath misting in the air. Every now and again, his bottle-top eyes flickered towards her before quickly staring straight ahead again. If she looked very closely, Blessing could even see how his mouth moved just a little each time he exhaled. He was like one of the guards at Buckingham Palace, except he did not have a red coat or a bearskin hat, and he was not nearly so good at keeping perfectly still.

'I can see you breathing, Mr Snowman.'

The snowman stopped breathing then. Blessing could

tell because his mouth was no longer moving.

And so she waited.

Sure enough, the snowman's bottle-tops soon began to flicker back and forth to Blessing with an ever-increasing urgency. After a few moments of this, the snowman coughed, gasped in a very deep breath and then held it once more.

'You're being ridiculous!' said Blessing. 'I already saw you stretch. And I saw your eyes move, and I can see you breathing, and I heard you cough. And look – these are your footprints!'

The snowman glanced his bottle-tops downwards, then quickly stared straight ahead again.

Blessing looked at him and shook her head.

There was really only one thing left to do.

So she took a very deep breath of her own, stood up on her tiptoes and yelled in the place where the snowman's ear would have been – if he had ears, which he didn't – just as loudly as she could.

'Excuse me!' she shouted. 'Can you hear me?'

The snowman now turned to look directly at Blessing.

'There is really no reason to raise your voice with me!' he said. He seemed quite cross.

'Oh,' said Blessing. 'Well, why didn't you answer me before?'

'Because of the Snowman Code, of course!' said the snowman.

'What's that?' asked Blessing.

'Don't tell me you've never heard of the Snowman Code?'

'I've never heard of the Snowman Code.'

'But then how did you know to speak to me six times?' asked the snowman.

'I didn't know to do that,' said Blessing. 'And, anyway, why is six times important?'

'Because,' explained the snowman, 'the Snowman Code says that we must always ignore humans the first five times they talk to us, but on the sixth time we are obliged to answer them.'

'Why are you obliged to answer us on the sixth time?' asked Blessing.

'Because it's only polite, of course!' answered the snowman.

Blessing frowned. Snowmen weren't supposed to know that it was important to be polite. After all, they weren't even supposed to be able to talk.

'Well, who invented this Snowman Code?' asked Blessing.

'What do you mean, who "invented" the Snowman Code?' said the snowman. 'Nobody invented it! It has been around since the days of Gurk himself!'

'Who was Gurk?' asked Blessing.

'Who was Gurk?' repeated the snowman incredulously. 'Don't tell me you don't know who Gurk was?'

'I don't know who Gurk was,' said Blessing.

'Gurk was the cave boy who built the very first snowman!'

'That must have been a long time ago,' said Blessing.

'It was!' agreed the snowman. 'It was many, many years ago. More even than nine!'

Blessing looked around in puzzlement. All the other things in the park – the ducks on the pond, the goalposts on the pitches, the swings in the playground – were still exactly where they were supposed to be, doing exactly what they were supposed to be doing. The only thing not doing what it was supposed to be doing was this snowman. Because snowmen really weren't meant to be able to talk. And, while any talking snowman would have been odd, this particular talking snowman seemed even odder still.

'What's your name?' asked Blessing.

'None of your business!' said the snowman.

'What's your name?' Blessing asked again.

'What?' said the snowman. 'I've just told you it's none of your business, and furthermore—'

'What's your name?' Blessing interrupted. 'What's your name? What's your name? Oh, and one more thing – what's your name?'

The snowman stared at Blessing.

'That's six,' she said, 'so now you have to tell me your name. It's the Snowman Code.'

'Fine,' huffed the snowman. 'In that case, my name is . . . er . . . Mr Frosty. Ahem. Ahem.'

Blessing noticed that the snowman had started to turn red.

'Mr Frosty, right. And how do you spell that?' Blessing asked.

'M-i-s—' began the snowman.

'I know how to spell Mister!' interrupted Blessing. 'I meant, how do you spell Frosty?'

'Ahem,' coughed the snowman. 'Well, it's f-o-r-s-s-t-i-e-y-i-e-e.'

The snowman paused there, and looked hopefully at Blessing. She seemed unimpressed, so he hastily added, 'And, of course, there's one more "e" on the end!'

Blessing only raised her eyebrows.

'And then maybe one last "e" after that?' said the

snowman, who had now turned very red indeed.

'No, that's not at all how you spell Frosty,' said Blessing. 'So why don't you just tell me your real name?'

The snowman shifted his bottle-tops down towards the ground.

'Because it isn't the kind of name that humans think snowmen should be called,' he said quietly.

'I don't care about that,' said Blessing.

'It's also a very old-fashioned sort of name,' said the snowman, 'and I am quite sensitive about it. So I will only tell you my name if you absolutely promise not to laugh.'

'I absolutely promise not to laugh,' said Blessing.

'Is that an ice promise?' asked the snowman, without looking up.

'Of course it is!' said Blessing, even though she had no idea what an ice promise was.

'Very well then,' said the snowman. 'My name is Albert Framlington.'

The snowman now raised his bottle-tops to look at

Blessing. He seemed to be waiting for her to laugh, but of course she did not. Only mean kids like the Driplet Triplets laughed at people's names.

Besides, she had made an ice promise. Whatever that was.

'You don't think Albert Framlington is a funny sort of a name for a snowman?' asked Albert Framlington.

'I think it's a very nice name for anybody,' said Blessing.

Albert Framlington seemed delighted by this.

'Well, that is something!' he said. 'That is something indeed! And now that you know my name, I suppose you'd better tell me your name too.'

'Of course,' she said. 'My name is Blessing.'

'I'm sorry,' he said, 'but could you say that again, please?'

'I said my name is Blessing.'

'Ha!' shouted Albert Framlington, and began to laugh so much that he had to hold his snowy sides.

'Hey!' said Blessing. 'What are you laughing about?'

'Your name!' he said. 'I've never heard such a funny name in all my winters!'

'That's very rude!' said Blessing. 'Especially after I was so nice about your name.'

Albert stopped laughing.

'I apologise,' he said, arranging his features into a serious expression. 'Article Seventeen of the Snowman Code says that we must never be rude. No matter how hilarious a thing might be.'

'Excuse me!' said Blessing. 'My name is not hilarious.'

'Exactly,' said Albert Framlington and held out his hand. 'And I'm entirely pleased to meet you, Blessing.' But, as he said her name, an unmistakable grin spread back across his face.

'I'm mostly pleased to meet you, Albert Framlington,' said Blessing and grudgingly shook his hand. It felt very cold because, after all, it was made of snow.

Just then, an icy gust of wind blew across the park. Blessing realised that not even Art Club went on this late.

'Well, Albert, I should be getting home,' she said.

'Good evening, then,' said Albert.

'Good evening,' said Blessing.

When she was halfway to the park gate, she heard Albert shout after her.

'Blessing! Please don't tell anyone that I'm alive!'

'Of course I won't!' Blessing shouted back. 'It's the Snowman Code!'

'It's not the Snowman Code!' Albert shouted after her. 'And anyway the Snowman Code only applies to snowmen!'

But Blessing did not hear him because she was already over the gate and heading home.

That night, Margaret cooked Blessing her very favourite dinner of home-made pizza.

At least, she tried to. Being sad sometimes made Margaret forgetful, and tonight she had forgotten to add the tomato sauce.

And home-made pizza without tomato sauce isn't really home-made pizza at all.

It's just home-made cheese on toast.

And home-made cheese on toast is just cheese on toast.

Still, Blessing reassured her mum that it was the most delicious home-made pizza that she had ever tasted.

'That's nice, dear,' replied Margaret.

As they ate, Blessing told Margaret all about her entirely made-up day at school. There had been a maths test, and an assembly about being careful when you cross the road, and then in the afternoon the class hamster had escaped.

'That's nice, dear,' said Margaret.

Of course, there was nothing especially nice about a maths test, an assembly about being careful when you cross the road or an escaped hamster. Blessing suspected Margaret was not really listening to her.

'Oh, and on my way home I met a snowman called

Albert Framlington. He told me about the Snowman Code. It goes all the way back to the days of Gurk.'

'That's nice, dear,' said Margaret.

Tucked up in her warm bed that night, Blessing heard Margaret turn on the radio in her bedroom next door. Margaret liked to listen to the radio in the long winter evenings because it made her feel less lonely. Blessing liked to hear her mum listen to the radio for the same reason.

As she drifted off to sleep, Blessing found herself wondering if Albert Framlington ever got cold and lonely out there, all by himself on the pitches in Victoria Park. She decided that, being a snowman, he probably at least did not get cold. But of course being lonely was quite bad enough.

And it wasn't as if Albert Framlington could even look forward to the bright summer evenings with kids yelling

and dogs barking and old people creaking and sprinklers hissing.

After all, as a snowman, he would surely melt as soon as spring came.

Three

The next morning, Blessing set off through Victoria Park. She checked to make sure nobody was nearby, then hurried across the pitches to Albert Framlington.

'Good morning!' she called out as she got close.

But Albert Framlington did not respond.

'Come on, Albert!' said Blessing. 'If I have to say everything six times, we're going to waste an awful lot of time.'

Albert did not reply but raised one twig eyebrow towards the far side of the pitches, where a jogger had just rounded the corner.

'Sorry!' whispered Blessing. 'I didn't see her!'

But Albert remained silent, and Blessing noticed his mouth had stopped moving.

'Why are you holding your breath?' she asked. 'I already know you're alive.'

Albert now raised both his twig eyebrows by just enough that you'd only ever notice it if you already knew snowmen were perfectly capable of raising their twig eyebrows.

'Oh,' said Blessing. 'There's somebody behind me, isn't there?'

Thwump!

Blessing found herself lying face down in the snow.

When she looked up, she saw exactly what she had known she would.

The Driplet Triplets.

'Why are you wearing your uniform when you don't even go to our school any more?' demanded Ashby Tregdahornick.

'Yeah, nobody likes you here, so you're supposed to be moving to Australia to be friends with kangaroos!' added Cynthia Smith-Smith.

'Kangaroos!' confirmed Bartholomew Weaselton.

It always went like this.

Ashby Tregdahornick said something mean.

Cynthia Smith-Smith said something even worse.

And then Bartholomew Weaselton agreed with them both.

'I'm still moving to Australia,' Blessing reassured them as she picked herself up from the snow. 'I just like to wear my uniform because I get nostalgic for all the good times we've had together.'

'Don't use French words at us!' yelled Ashby Tregdahornick. 'And who were you talking to just now, anyway?'

'Because it looked like you were talking to this snowman,' added Cynthia Smith-Smith.

'Snowman,' confirmed Bartholomew Weaselton.

Blessing did not care for the way the Driplet Triplets were looking at Albert Framlington. It made him seem very vulnerable. After all, he was only made of snow, and these three were absolute fiends.

'I was just talking to myself,' said Blessing. 'In French, of course. Because, well, I'm just completely mad like that. Or as I prefer to say it – *totalement folle*!'

But Blessing could see that Ashby Tregdahornick did not believe her. Sure enough, he kicked at Albert Framlington's shins until a large chunk of snow flew off.

And now the other two Driplets moved towards Albert too.

They were going to demolish him.

'Don't!' shouted Blessing, and the Driplet Triplets turned to look at her.

'Why not?' Ashby Tregdahornick smirked.

'Yeah, give us one good reason why we shouldn't smash up your stupid snowman?' Cynthia Smith-Smith grinned.

'Snowman,' beamed Bartholomew Weaselton.

Of course, Blessing knew very well that any reason she gave them not to smash Albert up would only make the Driplet Triplets enjoy smashing him up even more.

Luckily, she was a lot smarter than them.

'No, I meant don't stop,' she said. 'Don't stop smashing that snowman up! And please, hurry up!'

Albert raised his twig eyebrows at Blessing in a discreet yet urgent manner. But Blessing knew exactly what she was doing.

Because the Driplet Triplets now stopped and stared at each other in confusion.

The whole point of smashing the snowman up had been to upset Blessing.

But she had just asked them not to stop smashing him up!

They were still staring at each other in bafflement when

the school bell rang in the distance. They turned to leave but, as they went, Ashby Tregdahornick grabbed Blessing's schoolbag from the ground.

'And why are you still carrying this around?' he demanded.

'You won't be needing that in Australia!' added Cynthia Smith-Smith.

'Australia!' echoed Bartholomew Weaselton.

As the Driplet Triplets departed across the pitches, Ashby Tregdahornick emptied Blessing's bag out on to the ground.

Her books.

Her pencil case.

Her sketchbook.

They made a trail in the snow, right to the bin, where Ashby Tregdahornick deposited her now empty bag.

Blessing kept her back turned to Albert as she gathered up

her things. She did not even like humans to see her cry, so she certainly did not want a snowman to do so.

When she did finally glance at him, Albert Framlington seemed like he was preparing to ask her about what had just happened. Luckily, right then a group of cross-country skiers came swishing past them, and Blessing followed them out of the park.

Four

Blessing took the bus across town to the big museum, but everything today felt wrong. There were no school trips for her to join, and even the giant stuffed walrus had been taken away to have his tusks polished. She then went to Leicester Square and tried to sneak into the matinee of a play, but an usher caught her. He told her that if she ever tried that again he would call the police, and they would probably send her to prison. Blessing did not believe him

on either count, but she would still rather he had not said such unpleasant things.

Even going to the cinema did not help! The movie being shown that day was about a brave young boy who saved a rare species of tree frog from extinction. It seemed like it might be a good movie, but the actor playing the hero looked a lot like Ashby Tregdahornick. It was quite impossible to believe that anybody that bore any resemblance to Ashby Tregdahornick was capable of ever doing anything nice, let alone saving a rare species of tree frog.

By mid-afternoon, Blessing found herself back in Victoria Park.

She talked to the ducks, and swung on the swings, but eventually she found herself walking past Albert Framlington.

'Good afternoon, Blessing!' called out Albert.

'Oh, hello,' said Blessing. 'What are you doing here?'

'What in glaciers do you mean, what am I doing here?' asked Albert. 'I live here.'

Blessing shrugged. 'I must have forgotten.'

Albert Framlington went quiet then, and Blessing saw he'd arranged his twig eyebrows into a frown. She could tell he was preparing to ask her about the Driplet Triplets, so instead she quickly asked him the first question that came to her mind.

'Don't you ever get lonely out here?'

'Lonely? Me? Snowstorms, no!' Albert said. 'In fact, I have entirely the opposite problem!'

'What? What do you mean, the opposite problem?' asked Blessing.

'Far too much company!' explained Albert. 'Because do you know that snowman that lives near the West Entrance?'

Blessing did know the snowman that Albert was talking about.

He was a 10/10 snowman.

He had pieces of coal for eyes.

A carrot for a nose.

A pipe in his mouth.

He even had a deerstalker hat and a tweed jacket.

And he was not in the slightest bit lopsided.

'I've seen him,' said Blessing. 'He has a pipe and—'

'Well, his name is Jeremiah,' interrupted Albert. 'And he is forever coming over here and talking to me. So I'm not lonely at all. But if I ever was I could go over there and talk to him. Though of course I don't want to do that.'

'Why not?' asked Blessing.

'Because he never stops talking about his pipe! I mean, from the way he goes on about it, you'd think he was the first snowman in history to ever have had a pipe!'

For the first time that day, Blessing found herself smiling.

'Albert,' she asked, 'is the reason you don't like that other snowman because he has a pipe and you don't?'

'It's not even a real pipe,' continued Albert. 'Because

that whole outfit he wears is from a fancy-dress shop. It's a Sherlock Holmes costume. He was a very famous zookeeper, by the way.'

'Sherlock Holmes wasn't a zookeeper,' said Blessing. 'He was the most famous detective who ever lived.'

'Hmmmm,' Albert frowned. 'I think you'll find he was a zookeeper. But anyway, that's not the point.'

'Then what is the point?' asked Blessing.

'The point is it's not a real pipe! And do you know something else? From the way Jeremiah goes on about it, I think he was probably born in summer!'

Albert rolled his bottle-top eyes as he said this. Blessing got the impression he thought being born in the summer was the most ridiculous thing imaginable.

'What's wrong with being born in the summer?' she asked.

'You really don't know?'

'I really don't know,' said Blessing.

'It's how we snowmen insult each other. After all, being

born in summer – can you imagine anything worse?'

'Yes, I can,' said Blessing, 'because I was born in the summer. And I quite like it, actually.'

Albert stared at Blessing, and then slowly nodded.

'Yes.' He sighed. 'Yes, I suppose that does make sense.'

'What?' asked Blessing. 'What do you mean, "that does make sense"?'

'Well, for instance, you didn't know that Sherlock Holmes was a famous zookeeper, and you hadn't even heard of Gurk,' said Albert. 'But your secret about being born in summer is safe with me!'

'It's not a secret,' said Blessing. 'My birthday is in July and I don't care who knows it.'

'Shhhh!' cautioned Albert. 'I really wouldn't go spreading that around if I were you.'

Blessing decided it was best to change the subject.

'So what do you do out here all day, anyway?' she asked.

'Oh, I mostly sleep,' Albert said, 'because we snowmen are nocturnal.'

'Snowmen are nocturnal?' asked Blessing.

'It means we sleep during the day and are awake all night,' said Albert.

'I know what nocturnal means!' said Blessing. 'I just didn't know that snowmen are nocturnal.'

'Well, of course we are!' said Albert, proudly puffing his chest out. 'In fact, we are the only nocturnal marsupials.'

'A marsupial is an animal that carries its offspring in a pouch,' said Blessing.

'Well, we certainly don't do that,' said Albert. 'But we are definitely the only nocturnal marsupials. We're famous for it!'

'Maybe you're thinking of possums?' suggested Blessing.

'Maybe you should look it up in an encyclopedia,' said Albert. 'That's a sort of dictionary of animals.'

'If you say so,' said Blessing. 'But if you're nocturnal, what do you do all night?'

Albert looked concerned for a moment, and then his bottle-tops lit up.

'I go to the cinema! I eat cornpop and I listen to the orchestra and afterwards I wait at the stage door so I can shake the actors' hands and congratulate them on their fine performances! Ahem!'

'Really?' asked Blessing.

'Absolutely!' said Albert.

'So what's your favourite kind of film to watch?' asked Blessing.

'The kind that has a lot of flowers in it,' replied Albert.

'That's not an actual kind of film,' said Blessing.

'Of course it is!' said Albert. 'The two kinds of films are films with a lot of flowers in them, and films with not enough flowers. I'm surprised you don't know that. Haven't you ever been to the cinema? Ahem.'

Blessing looked at Albert. Sure enough, he had started to go a little red.

'Isn't there anything in the Snowman Code about telling fibs?' she asked.

'What in the blizzards makes you think I am telling fibs?' asked Albert. 'Ahem, ahem.'

'I know you're telling fibs,' said Blessing, 'because those aren't real kinds of films, and that isn't even what happens when you go to the cinema.'

'Which part of it isn't what happens when you go to the cinema?' asked Albert.

'All of it,' said Blessing. 'And they don't divide them into films with and without flowers either.'

'Well, fine then,' said Albert Framlington. 'Maybe strictly speaking I've never actually been to the cinema. But I'd very much like to go. And that is exactly the same thing.'

'No, it isn't,' said Blessing. 'It's not the same thing at all.'

Albert did not reply, but turned away from Blessing and made a point of looking in every other possible direction.

He then started to quietly whistle to himself, and Blessing understood he was in a huff.

'Look, if you want to go to the cinema so much, why don't you just go to the cinema?'

'Because of the Snowman Code, of course,' explained Albert. 'Article Six says snowmen can't go anywhere without a disguise unless it is very late at night, and only then when it is very important. And I don't have a disguise this winter. So here I stay. With only Jeremiah and his pipe for company.'

'What kind of disguise would you need?' asked Blessing.

'Don't they teach children anything in school these days?' grumbled Albert, before seeming to perk up at the very thought of a disguise. 'A disguise consists of a hat, sunglasses, a nice clean scarf, gloves, a long coat, trousers and a good pair of wellington boots to catch any drips!'

Five

Blessing already had the sunglasses and a nice clean scarf in her dressing-up box. She bought the other things from the charity shop near her house with some of the money she had saved by eating leftover popcorn for lunch.

The next day, she took them all to Albert. They waited until there was nobody around, and then Albert quickly put them all on.

He looked just like a human!

A very pale human wearing far too many clothes.

And dark sunglasses in the middle of winter.

And wellington boots that were at least three sizes too big for him.

But a human, nonetheless.

Or at least enough of a human that nobody would give him a second glance. After all, lots of unusual-looking people lived in London. If you stopped to give them all second glances, you would never get anywhere.

Albert insisted that they leave the park by the West Entrance. Their route there took them past the Rose Garden, and when they reached it Albert stopped and peered inside.

'Are there really roses here in the summer?' he asked.

'Of course there are.' Blessing shrugged. 'It's a rose garden.'

'But just how many roses are we talking about here?' asked Albert. 'Surely not as many as seven or eight roses?'

'Hundreds,' said Blessing. 'Hundreds and hundreds.'

'Hundreds and hundreds of roses!' said Albert, getting a faraway look in his bottle-tops as he spoke. 'Imagine that! Hundreds and hundreds of roses, right in there during the summertime! That must be quite a sight.'

'It is,' said Blessing. 'But come on or we'll be late.'

They had not gone much further when Albert suddenly whispered, 'Freeze!' and stood stock-still. Blessing braced herself for whatever terrible thing the Driplet Triplets were about to do to her. But nothing happened, and when Blessing turned around she saw that the park was completely empty apart from a small dog trotting past the duck pond in the far distance.

'Why did you tell me to freeze?' asked Blessing. 'There's nobody there.'

'Nobody there?' whispered Albert urgently. 'There's a dog!'

'I didn't know you were scared of dogs,' said Blessing.

'Well, of course I'm not scared of them!' said Albert, who had still not moved so much as a single snowflake. 'We snowmen just don't like them at all.'

'Why don't snowmen like dogs?' asked Blessing.

'They started it,' said Albert. 'So you'd really have to ask them.'

'Come on,' said Blessing. 'He's gone now. He was only little, anyway.'

'Those little ones are the most dangerous of all,' muttered Albert.

When they reached the West Entrance, Albert asked Blessing to wait for a moment, and walked over to say something to Jeremiah. Blessing thought she saw Jeremiah's carrot nose wrinkle, and so when Albert came back she asked him what he had said.

'Oh, nothing important,' said Albert. 'I just told him that I was going to the cinema. But he shouldn't feel at all jealous because after all he has that wonderful pipe.'

The bus went from just outside the park to the front door of the cinema, so getting there was simple enough. At least, it would have been simple enough if Albert Framlington had ever ridden on a bus before. He insisted on shaking hands with the driver and all the other passengers, and one woman told him that his hand was so cold he must see a doctor immediately. He then lay down across the entire back seat as if it was a bed, closed his eyes and told Blessing to wake him up when they were coming in to land.

Blessing explained that this was not how buses worked, and Albert needed to sit up and look quietly out of the window like everybody else. When they reached their stop, Albert rang the bell until the bus driver shouted at them.

Albert was much too big to fit through the toilet window at the cinema, so Blessing bought him a ticket, then climbed through the window herself. She found Albert in the corridor staring intently at a poster. When she asked him what he was doing, he shushed her and told her it was very rude to talk during the film. It took

Blessing a long time to convince Albert that the poster was not the film. Even as they walked away from it, he kept glancing back over his shoulder to make sure he was not missing anything important.

The actual film playing that day was a cartoon about a talking vacuum cleaner. Blessing thought it was ridiculous, but Albert said it was the greatest movie he had ever seen.

They watched it a second time, and then a third time. Albert even asked if they could watch it a fourth time, but Blessing said no, she needed to get back home.

Albert admitted that was probably just as well, because if he stayed much longer he might begin to melt. Sure

enough, when they got up to leave, there were two wet footprints beneath Albert's seat.

On the bus back home, the other passengers were all talking loudly about how much longer this winter might go on for. One of them said that the last great winter had occurred in the year 1773, and back then the snow had lain on the ground until May. Another passenger said you could not compare then to now, because nowadays the weather was broken.

Overhearing these conversations about the broken weather reminded Blessing of something that had been troubling her.

'Albert,' she asked, 'what happens after the snow melts?'

'Oh, my sweet summer child!' Albert laughed. 'What happens after the snow melts is that winter ends and then it is the next season, which is called spring.'

'I know the seasons!' said Blessing. 'I meant what

happens to you when the snow melts?'

'Oh,' said Albert. 'Well, I melt too, of course.'

Blessing had expected this, but nonetheless she suddenly felt very sad indeed. She turned away from Albert and stared out of the window. Outside, the busy people of London were starting to make their way home from school or work or wherever it was they went all day. It seemed unfair that none of them had to worry about melting when spring came.

They travelled on quite a way before Albert spoke again.

'I don't die, though, if that is what you're thinking,' he said.

This was exactly what Blessing was thinking, so Albert's words sent her heart up into her mouth.

'You really don't die?' she whispered, worried that Albert might think 'dying' meant visiting the zoo or drinking a glass of milk or who knows what else.

'Of course I don't die! That would be far too sad! Hundreds of thousands of snowmen dying every spring? No, no, no! That would be a snowy catastrophe!'

'So what happens to you when spring comes?' asked Blessing.

'Article Nine of the Snowman Code decrees we must hold a great big party to mark the end of winter. So what happens to me when spring comes is that I go to a great big party and have a wonderful time.'

'But after the party? What happens to you after the party?'

'Do you know the most incredible fact about Planet Earth?' asked Albert. 'It is that it is always snowing somewhere! So, even as the snow is melting here in London, it is beginning to fall somewhere else. And you must surely know what that means?'

Blessing shook her head.

'It means,' said Albert, 'that somewhere else on Earth there is always a child building a snowman!'

Blessing looked only more confused.

'Oh, it's really very simple,' explained Albert. 'After I melt here, I wake up somewhere else in a beautiful new

body of fresh snow that a child has kindly just built for me.'

'You melt here, and you wake up as another snowman – just like that?' asked Blessing.

'Of course!' said Albert. 'Haven't you ever heard the saying, "Snowmen go north in the summer"?'

'That's birds!' said Blessing. 'And they go south in the winter.'

'Then the birds must have copied it from us,' said Albert. 'Anyway, even you must at least have heard that snowmen have nine lives?'

'That's cats!' said Blessing.

'Absolute icicles!' said Albert. 'It's snowmen!'

'Fine,' said Blessing. 'It's snowmen. But does that mean you can only melt nine times?'

'Of course not!' said Albert. 'We can melt endless times. It's just that nine is as big a number as anybody can reasonably be expected to count to.'

'No, it's not,' said Blessing. 'I'm only ten and a half and I can count to—'

Albert burst out into the kind of laughter that made him grab his snowy sides.

'What?' asked Blessing. 'What's so funny now?'

'If you're only ten-and-a-half winters, it's really no wonder you don't know anything!'

'Excuse me!' said Blessing. 'I'm not only ten-and-a-half winters, I'm ten-and-a-half winters and summers!'

'Well, I suppose that is a little better,' said Albert. 'You see, all this moving from one winter place to another means we snowmen live two or three winters for every human year. So, if you were a snowman, you'd be twenty or thirty winters old by now. But even that is still very young, so it's really no surprise you know so little!'

'Actually,' said Blessing, 'I know a lot more than you! I know what a marsupial is and what an encyclopedia is, and that Sherlock Holmes was a detective, and I know how to speak French and—'

'You didn't even know that snowmen go north in the summer!' interrupted Albert.

'Because that's not snowmen! That's birds! And they go south in the winter!'

'Well, you also didn't even know that snowmen have nine lives,' said Albert.

'Because that's also not snowmen! That's cats!' said Blessing.

The other passengers on the bus had started to turn round and look at them. Blessing realised she had been shouting and lowered her voice.

'How old are you, anyway?' she asked.

'Six hundred and twenty-seven winters!' said Albert proudly.

'That's a lot of winters,' said Blessing, sounding more impressed than she had intended to.

'It is! And in that time I have been a snowman all across the world! In France, I was a snowman at a monastery high in the Alps. In Russia, I was a snowman to the court of the tsar. In China, I was a snowman atop the Great Wall. In America, I was a Hollywood snowman, that is to say, a snowman to the stars. I was even a snowman in Africa once. Oh, that

was one of the best and longest winters I've ever had.'

'Which part of Africa was that?' asked Blessing.

'What does it matter which part of Africa it was?' said Albert.

'It's just that Africa isn't really known for having a lot of snow or long winters,' explained Blessing.

'Africa isn't known for having a lot of snow?' exclaimed Albert. 'My sweet summer child, Africa is famous throughout the world for its snow! And it is almost always winter in Africa!'

'Are you sure about that?' asked Blessing.

'Haven't you ever seen pictures of Africa?' asked Albert. 'It is nothing but snow and ice and penguins and the South Pole!'

'You don't mean Africa,' said Blessing. 'You mean Antarctica.'

'Well, however you want to pronounce it,' sniffed Albert, 'I was a snowman there.'

When they reached their stop, Albert once again rang the bell until the driver shouted at them.

Six

Albert insisted they re-enter the park by the West Entrance, even though it was a longer walk. He claimed this was to make sure they did not get lost on the way back to the pitches, but Blessing suspected it was because he wanted another chance to rub Jeremiah's carrot in it.

But as they entered the park, Jeremiah lifted his deerstalker hat and cheerfully waved it at them.

'I hope you enjoyed yourselves,' he called out. 'I've

been having the most wonderful time smoking my pipe.'

'You haven't been smoking it because it isn't a real pipe,' Albert called back.

'That's not very nice, Albert,' whispered Blessing.

'Yes, much better!' Jeremiah called back to Albert. 'Thank you very much for asking!'

Albert did not correct Jeremiah, but only rolled his bottle-tops and carried on walking.

'What was that about?' asked Blessing.

'We snowmen don't have the best hearing,' explained Albert. 'A few snowmen claim it is because we do not have any ears, but I don't believe that can possibly be true.'

'Why not?' asked Blessing.

'I think I would have heard a lot more about it,' said Albert.

As they passed the bin where Ashby Tregdahornick had deposited her schoolbag, Blessing noticed Albert's twigs arrange themselves into a frown. She had an idea of what he was going to say, and quickly tried to think of another

question with which to distract him, but she was too late.

'Blessing,' he said, 'one reason why we snowmen sometimes get complicated things like Africa and Antarctica muddled up is because we don't get to go to school.'

'Oh.' Blessing shrugged.

'And I really would have liked to go to school,' said Albert. 'So that makes me wonder why you don't go?'

'It's the holidays,' said Blessing. 'So there isn't any school at the moment.'

'Right,' said Albert. 'But the thing is, that's not really true, is it? Because all the other children are still going to school. I see them in their uniforms every day.'

Blessing did not say anything, but carried on walking.

'If you won't tell me why you don't go to school,' said Albert, 'I'll just ask you six times, and then you'll have to tell me. It's the Snowman Code.'

'I'm not a snowman,' said Blessing. 'So the Snowman Code doesn't apply to me.'

'Well, maybe you should tell me, anyway,' said Albert.

'If there is some sort of problem that stops you going to school, I'd like to help you with it.'

'You can't possibly help me,' said Blessing.

Albert stopped walking and turned to look at Blessing in astonishment. 'Whatever makes you think I can't help you?' he asked.

Blessing gestured at, well, all of him.

'You think I can't help you because I'm a snowman?' Albert asked. 'But that's exactly why I can help you! It's Article Two of the Snowman Code: "A snowman always helps a child in need."'

'I'm not a child in need!' said Blessing.

'Of course you aren't,' said Albert. 'My mistake.'

They walked on a bit in silence, and then Albert spoke again.

'It's just – well, are you quite sure that you are not a child in need? We snowmen do tend to have a sense for these things.'

Blessing turned her head away and stared at the duck

pond. Sometimes people being kind to her was harder to deal with than people being mean.

'It's those three children from the other day, isn't it? They are why you don't go to school.'

'Might be them.' Blessing shrugged. 'Might not be.'

'But the thing is, if it was them,' said Albert, 'then I could definitely help you!'

'How? How could you help me?'

Albert glanced around to make sure nobody was nearby, then lowered his voice.

'Once, I was a snowman in India,' he said. 'And there was a very bad man who lived in our village. He was a terrible bully, and he made everybody's life a misery. He was so wicked that when the police tried to arrest him, he just bullied them too! But then guess what happened?'

'He carried on bullying everyone and got away with it forever.'

'No!' said Albert. 'He was eaten by a tiger! Completely

eaten right up! Nothing whatsoever left of him except his trousers!'

Albert's features had arranged themselves into a triumphant grin.

'You see!' he said. 'I told you I could help you!'

'What are you talking about?' asked Blessing. 'How does that help me?'

'Oh, my sweet summer child!' Albert laughed. 'Isn't it obvious? You just have to obtain a man-eating tiger!'

A moment of silence fell on the park as Blessing tried to count to ten in the way her mum had taught her to do anytime something made her really cross. She got as far as seven before she could hold it no longer.

'Albert Framlington!' she shouted. 'Your great plan to help me deal with the Driplet Triplets is that I find a tiger and have them eaten?'

'Are you saying that you don't think it's a very good plan?' asked Albert.

'I'm saying it's the worst plan I have ever heard!' said Blessing.

'Yes, I can see now that it might be somewhat impractical,' admitted Albert. 'It would be hard to obtain a good tiger here. I suppose we could enquire at the zoo, but it's quite unlikely even they would have a reliable man-eater available at short notice.'

'I knew you couldn't help me,' said Blessing.

'But I have to help you!' said Albert. 'It's the Snowman Code. So just let me think! Let me think again!'

Blessing watched as Albert rubbed his potato nose.

Rubbing their nose is what snowmen do when they think. It does not matter whether their nose is a potato or a carrot or a broken lollipop stick. Rubbing it helps them think.

At least, they believe it helps them think, which is of course actually the important thing.

After a few moments, Blessing thought she saw a little bit of steam come out of the place where Albert's

ears would have been. Before she could ask him about it, Albert slapped his forehead so hard that it sent a few tiny snowflakes fluttering off from it.

'Great glaciers!' he exclaimed. 'I've got it! A much better idea! Not even somebody born in summer could mess this one up!'

'This had better be good,' said Blessing.

Albert looked around them once more, and this time he lowered his voice to a whisper so quiet that Blessing had to lean in close to hear him.

'Have you ever heard of the Abominable Snowman?' he asked.

This idea was so ridiculous that Blessing did not even need to count to ten.

'Of course I've heard of the Abominable Snowman,' she said. 'He's a made-up giant snow monster who is supposed to live in the mountains of Tibet.'

'What do you mean, "made-up"?' frowned Albert.

'I mean he isn't real,' replied Blessing.

'The Abominable Snowman, not real? Of course the Abominable Snowman is real!' said Albert. 'I mean, you didn't even think I could be real until recently, did you? And yet here I am!'

'Fine,' said Blessing. 'So tell me about him.'

'Well, the first thing to know about the Abominable Snowman,' explained Albert, 'is that he does not actually live in the mountains of Tibet. Everybody always gets that wrong about him, including many people who weren't even born in summer. In fact, the Abominable Snowman lives here, in London.'

'Whereabouts in London?' asked Blessing.

'Right here in Victoria Park,' said Albert.

'Albert, if you mean Jeremiah—' began Blessing.

'I don't mean Jeremiah!' interrupted Albert. 'Yes, Jeremiah is a snowman, and quite abominable in his own way, but he is not the Abominable Snowman.'

'If the Abominable Snowman lived in this park, there'd be signs up to warn people. I'd have noticed footprints in

the snow. I might even have seen him—'

'But you have seen him!' interrupted Albert. 'You are talking to him right now!'

Blessing gave Albert a look intended to let him know this was the most ridiculous thing she had ever heard.

But then Albert Framlington stood up taller, shrugged his shoulders up and pulled his mouth into a wide grimace.

He did suddenly look quite fearsome.

And then he growled.

And, even though it was a quiet growl, it was tremendously powerful.

And quite terrifying.

After all, it was exactly the kind of growl that the Abominable Snowman would make if he was hungry.

'That's incredible!' whispered Blessing.

'I know!' said Albert proudly. 'I learned that growl from a tiger in India. That man-eater I told you about.'

Seven

The next day, Blessing sat on a bench outside the Rose Garden that she knew the Driplet Triplets would walk by after school finished. It was on the way to the canal, and they went there every afternoon to shout at the swans.

Sure enough, at four o'clock, they arrived.

'Well, look what's still here,' said Ashby Tregdahornick.

'Seems like somebody didn't learn her lesson on

Wednesday!' added Cynthia Smith-Smith.

'Wednesday!' agreed Bartholomew Weaselton.

'I'm sorry,' said Blessing. 'I hope you can forgive me. The thing is, I'm only here because I have a leaving present for you.'

This confused the Driplet Triplets. They had always been awful to Blessing, so deep down they knew there was no reason whatsoever for her to give them any kind of present.

And yet – they might get a present!

The thing about bullies is that they are never very bright, but they are almost always very greedy.

'So where is this present?' asked Ashby Tregdahornick.

'It had better be a good present,' said Cynthia Smith-Smith.

'Present!' confirmed Bartholomew Weaselton.

'It's in there,' said Blessing, pointing through the stone archway that led into the Rose Garden.

The Driplet Triplets looked at each other uneasily.

Nobody ever went in the Rose Garden in winter. There was no reason to do so, because there were no roses in winter.

And yet – they might get a present!

So the other two Driplets now did what they always did when they were not sure about something, which was to stare expectantly at Ashby Tregdahornick.

And Ashby Tregdahornick did what he always did when the other two Driplets stared at him like that, which was to hiss, 'Stop staring at me! I'm thinking!'

'It's only in there because I wanted it to be a special surprise you could remember me by,' Blessing explained. 'Whenever you think of me in the future, I want you to remember—'

Blessing stopped talking. She could already see by their faces that she had overdone it. And, sure enough, Ashby Tregdahornick started to walk away, and the other two Driplets followed.

Blessing felt a familiar sadness creep over her then. So

much for the Abominable Snowman and Albert's cunning plan!

The next time Blessing saw the Driplet Triplets, nothing would have changed.

They would still be calling her names and emptying her things out into the snow.

She still would not be able to go to school.

But wait! When he was halfway to the lane that led to the canal, Ashby Tregdahornick stopped and looked back towards the Rose Garden. And, because he did that, so too did Cynthia Smith-Smith and Bartholomew Weaselton.

'We should probably get our present,' said Ashby Tregdahornick.

'We've certainly earned it,' said Cynthia Smith-Smith.

'Earned it!' agreed Bartholomew Weaselton.

The Rose Garden was enclosed by high stone walls. In summer, it bloomed with hundreds of bright-coloured,

sweet-smelling flowers that entirely covered them. By midsummer, the roses even climbed all the way across a net that hung between the walls, to make a kind of canopy of roses.

But that was all in summertime.

In winter, the Rose Garden was a different kind of place entirely. The rose bushes lost all their pretty flowers and kept only their thorns. The stone walls stood bare and cold. And the empty net above you made you feel like you were in some kind of prison. Of course, this was exactly why Blessing had chosen it.

'There's your present,' she told the Driplet Triplets after she had followed them in through the stone archway. 'I hope you like him.'

Blessing was pointing at Albert.

The Driplet Triplets stared at him in furious disbelief.

He was exactly the same lifeless, lopsided, 3/10, bottle-tops-for-eyes and small-old-potato-for-a-nose snowman that he had always been. The only difference was that

he was now in the Rose Garden.

'A snowman isn't a present and you didn't even make him!' spluttered Ashby Tregdahornick.

'All you've done is move him in here from the pitches!' shouted Cynthia Smith-Smith.

'Pitches!' yelled Bartholomew Weaselton.

'Shhhh!' Blessing cautioned. 'You don't want to wake him. Because that's not just any old snowman. Your present there – he's the Abominable Snowman!'

'There's no such thing as the Abominable Snowman,' barked Ashby Tregdahornick.

'And he lives in Tibet, anyway!' bellowed Cynthia Smith-Smith.

'Tibet!' screeched Bartholomew Weaselton.

'We're going to bash you up!' thundered Ashby Tregdahornick.

'And then we're going to smash your stupid snowman up!' screamed Cynthia Smith-Smith.

'Up!' shrieked Bartholomew Weaselton.

As the Driplet Triplets began to advance on her, Blessing walked backwards until the cold stone wall behind her told her there was nowhere else to go.

She looked across to Albert, but he had not moved so much as a snowflake. And still the Driplet Triplets continued coming for her.

'Albert!' whispered Blessing urgently. 'Albert!'

Albert did not react, and Blessing thought he must have fallen asleep.

Even allowing for the fact that snowmen are nocturnal, this was a bit much.

But right as the Driplet Triplets drew back their fists there came a low growl.

It wasn't loud.

But it was tremendously powerful.

And quite terrifying.

It sounded exactly like the kind of growl a man-eating tiger might make if you had disturbed his nap and he'd woken up hungry.

Slowly, the Driplet Triplets turned around.

And there, right behind them, was the Abominable Snowman!

He was standing taller than Blessing had ever seen him stand before.

He leaned forward, so that he blocked out the winter sun, and the three Driplet Triplets were in his shadow.

He raised both his arms up high to the sky.

And now he roared.

How the Abominable Snowman roared!

The Abominable Snowman roared so loudly that Ashby Tregdahornick immediately wet himself.

Cynthia Smith-Smith burst into tears.

And Bartholomew Weaselton could only nod his head in agreement with both the wetting and the crying.

But it was when the Driplet Triplets tried to run away that the real fun started. Because the stone archway is the

only way out of the Rose Garden and, as they all ran for it, the three Driplet Triplets crashed into one another and tumbled to the ground. By the time they picked themselves up, the Abominable Snowman was blocking the archway. And then he began to chase them around the Rose Garden.

Around and around they went. Each time the Driplet Triplets ran into one another, they screamed. Each time they ran into the Abominable Snowman, they screamed even louder.

Blessing could not stop laughing. She was laughing so

hard she could not breathe. She knew this was wrong, and that it made her little better than them.

Still, it was hilarious! After all, the Driplet Triplets thought they were running away from the Abominable Snowman. But really it was just silly old Albert Framlington, a perfectly ordinary snowman who was even terrified of small dogs.

Eventually, Ashby Tregdahornick found his way out of the Rose Garden. He was soon followed by Cynthia Smith-Smith, and finally by Bartholomew Weaselton.

As he left, Bartholomew Weaselton turned to Blessing and gasped the only two original words she had ever heard him say.

'Abominable Snowman!'

After the Driplet Triplets had gone, Blessing ran over and hugged Albert.

'Thank you,' she whispered. 'Thank you so much!'

Albert's features arranged themselves into a wide grin. He seemed every bit as pleased as Blessing was that he had vanquished the Driplet Triplets.

'Do you think you can go back to school now?' he asked.

'Yes!' said Blessing. 'I'll just have to write another note to Miss Hazelworst and tell her that Australia was closed when we got there. You've helped me so much, Albert. I don't know how to thank you.'

'There's no need to thank me,' said Albert, 'because I was just doing my duty under the Snowman Code. Any snowman would have done exactly the same thing.'

'Maybe,' said Blessing. 'But I don't think they'd have had your brilliant idea to be the Abominable Snowman.'

'Well, that is very true,' said Albert. 'Very true indeed. Nonetheless, I will refuse to accept any medal you might try to award me, so don't even think of giving me one. Especially not a shiny gold one on a red ribbon.'

'You don't need to worry about that,' said Blessing. 'I don't even know where I'd get a gold medal.'

'Oh,' said Albert, who seemed a little disappointed. 'I see. Well, the Snowman Code is quite clear that we must help a child in need with all their problems, not just the first one they happen to mention. So is there anything else I can help you with? Perhaps something that might lead to the awarding of a gold medal on a red ribbon?'

The one thing Blessing did desperately need help with seemed too serious even for gold medals and red ribbons. It was her mum, and the fact that she was so sad. But if even Dr Kumar's lamp had not been able to make Margaret better, then the Abominable Snowman certainly could not help her.

'There isn't anything else you can help me with, Albert,' sighed Blessing. 'Not unless you can fix the broken weather and make this winter end.'

'Ahem.' Albert coughed. 'Ahem. Ahem.'

'What?' asked Blessing. 'What is it?'

'Nothing,' said Albert, who had begun to turn red. 'Ahem.'

'Then why have you turned red?'

'I haven't turned red,' said Albert. 'Ahem. Ahem.'

'You have!' said Blessing. 'You're bright red!'

'Well, it's a medical condition I have,' said Albert. 'So it is actually very rude of you to mention it.'

'Excuse me!' said Blessing. 'It's not a medical condition, is it? You always turn red when you fib, and you turned red after I said you couldn't make the winter end.'

'Ahem,' coughed Albert. 'Ahem. Ahem.'

'And you always cough like that when you're trying to hide something! So what is it?'

Blessing looked Albert straight in his bottle-tops, but he shifted them away from her eyes.

'Albert Framlington,' she said, 'do you or do you not know how to make this winter end?'

'Well, look—' he stammered. 'Ahem. I mean. It's technically possible that— I mean—'

'Albert!' shouted Blessing.

'The thing about it all,' said Albert, 'is that under Article

Five of the Snowman Code, winter is only permitted to end when all the snowmen in a place feel ready to melt. So it is possible the reason it is still winter is that somewhere in this city there is a snowman who perhaps does not yet feel quite ready to melt.'

Blessing stared at Albert in disbelief.

'Albert Framlington, are you telling me that this winter has gone on so long because one selfish snowman has refused to melt?'

'I wouldn't necessarily say it was selfish of this snowman,' said Albert. 'I'm sure he has his reasons. But all the rest of it—'

'Then we need to find him!' interrupted Blessing. 'We need to find him and make him melt right away!'

'Right, right, of course,' said Albert. 'But I just mean – is endless winter really so very bad?'

'Yes!' said Blessing. 'Endless winter really is so very bad!'

'But when you really think about it, I mean?' replied Albert.

'Especially when you really think about it! It's made my mum so unwell that I might get sent away again!'

'I'm sorry to hear that,' said Albert. 'I do hope they can fix her appendix.'

'What? What are you talking about, her appendix?'

'Appendicitis. It's the usual reason humans become unwell,' explained Albert. 'Such a mischievous little blighter, the appendix. I can't tell you how glad I am that we snowmen don't have such wretched things.'

'My mum isn't unwell because of her appendix!' said Blessing. 'She's unwell because she's very sad, because of this endless winter. And if it goes on much longer she'll get even sadder and I'll definitely get sent away. So we have to find this snowman and make him melt!'

'It might not be possible to find him,' said Albert. 'There must be thousands of snowmen in this city. And look, even if we did find him, he probably has some very good and perfectly understandable reasons for not wanting to melt— Ahem! Ahem! Ahem!'

Albert had turned redder than Blessing had ever seen him before.

She suddenly realised why.

'It's you, isn't it?' she said.

'What is me?' asked Albert, as innocently as he could.

'The snowman who refuses to melt! The one who's kept this winter going on so long!'

Albert shifted his bottle-tops to the ground, and then there was a long silence.

'I mean, he is not not me,' Albert said quietly.

'Albert! How could you do this to me? And to everyone else in London? And why aren't you ready to melt?'

Albert shook his head. 'It's a very long story,' he said. 'You probably don't have time to hear it.'

'Actually, I have until spring comes!' said Blessing. 'So I'm going to sit right here on this bench until you tell me the whole thing.'

And so there, on a bench in the Rose Garden, Albert told Blessing his story.

It was indeed a long story!

And yet at its heart it was very short, and very simple, the same way that all true stories are.

Eight

When Albert was still a young snowman of only nineteen winters, he had fallen in love with another young snowman right here in London. Her eyes were perfect pieces of coal, her nose was the most immaculate parsnip, she wore a red tartan scarf and she had a laugh like an avalanche. And yet almost none of those things had mattered to Albert. After all, the coal of your eyes and the parsnip of your nose and the tartan of your scarf are merely temporary decorations.

Only a laugh like an avalanche and a heart itself do not change from one winter to the next.

And this young snowman – her name was Clementine – had the most beautiful heart that Albert had ever known. She was kind and gentle and she loved all snowmen and humans and animals. Clementine even loved dogs, and snowmen and dogs are sworn enemies. Loving dogs is entirely unheard of in snowmen!

Better still, Clementine loved Albert just as much as he loved her. She loved him not merely for the pipe he had that winter – a real pipe that still smelled of tobacco – or even his fashionable top hat and greatcoat. Nor did she love him simply because he was sweet and kind, knew a lot of surprising facts and always followed the Snowman Code. No, deep down in her most frozen places, Clementine loved Albert because his heart was just as true and pure as hers.

And what a winter Clementine and Albert had spent together, in that wonderful year of 1773! In those olden

days, human children went to a lot more effort when it came to dressing their snowmen. Clementine and Albert had both been born wearing full disguises, and they could therefore go wherever they pleased.

And so they did!

They took chilly arm-in-arm strolls through Regent's Park.

They ice-skated on the frozen ponds at Hampstead Heath.

They saw every single pantomime playing in Covent Garden – and many of them they even saw twice!

On the longest night of the year, they climbed Primrose Hill, watched the sun slowly rise over London and finally admitted that they were in love with each other.

And a week or so later they brought in the New Year in Trafalgar Square, and when the bells of St Martin-in-the-Fields rang out midnight, they promised each other they would never, ever part.

But, of course, the next day it was already January.

And soon after that it was February, and the humans who lived in London were already beginning to complain that winter had gone on too long.

And then it was March, and the humans were really complaining.

By April, the humans were all telling each other it was the longest winter since records began. (Records had only begun a few years earlier, so this did not mean very much, but the humans nonetheless loved to talk about them.)

And then the newspapers started to write that the only possible explanation for such a long winter was that Uruguay had cast a spell on Britain's weather. And therefore the only possible solution was to hold a war with Uruguay! A war would cause many young humans to lose their lives, but the older humans all agreed that it would be worth it to end the winter, and also to teach Uruguay a lesson.

Of course, Albert and Clementine knew that the problem

was not that Uruguay had cast a spell on Britain's weather. And they could not possibly let such a misunderstanding cost the lives of so many young humans.

And so, one dark night in May, they agreed the time had come to let themselves melt. The next time they woke up they would be in different bodies in different places.

And yet it was not the end of the world. Back then, only a few years after records had begun, our planet had seemed a lot smaller.

There were fewer places where children lived.

There were fewer places still where children lived that had snow at the same time.

And even fewer places still where children lived that had snow at the same time and where the children knew how to build a snowman.

Albert and Clementine therefore believed that soon – maybe even next winter, and at most after only another two or three had passed – they would once again find themselves in the same place. To make certain they would

not miss each other, they made an ice promise: at midnight, on the longest night of the year, they would always climb to the highest point of whatever city they were in, and there they would be reunited.

And so, the next morning, Albert and Clementine held hands as the sun came up.

And with that, the great winter of 1773 was suddenly over! The morning air was so warm that the snow melted almost immediately, and the young people danced in the streets, overjoyed that they would not have to go and fight the Uruguayans. After all, Uruguay was very far away, and anyway they did not want to lose their lives for no real reason.

Back in the Rose Garden, Albert stopped talking, yawned and stretched.

'Well, that's the end of the story,' he said, 'and you should probably be getting home now.'

'Wait!' said Blessing, who was trying very hard not to cry. 'Then what happened?'

'Nothing happened,' said Albert. 'That's the end of the story. Ahem.'

'No, it's not!' said Blessing. 'What happened next? What happened next with Clementine?'

Albert sighed and continued with the story.

What happened next was the world suddenly became a lot bigger.

Soon there were a lot more places where humans lived.

And each of them contained ever more children.

Ever more children building ever more snowmen.

And though, on the longest night of the year, Albert always climbed to the top of the highest hill in whatever village or town or city he found himself in, Clementine was never there.

And so one winter went by.

And then another.

And another.

And still Albert and Clementine did not find each other.

In every new place Albert found himself, he searched for Clementine. He asked every snowman he encountered if they had seen her. When they told him they had not, he made them promise to listen out for the sound of a laugh like an avalanche. And, when the longest night of the year came, Albert always climbed hopefully to the top of the highest hill of whatever city he was in.

Mount Atago in Kyoto.

Shankaracharya Hill in Srinigar.

Maungawhau in Auckland.

But Clementine was never there.

Still, as the winters went on, Albert heard occasional rumours of her.

In St Petersburg, a child told him about a snowman she had played with out on the steppe who had been friendly with a dog.

In Kathmandu, he met a snowman who claimed she had known a Clementine in Saskatoon the previous winter.

In Ulaanbaatar, he even met an Outer Mongolian snowman who said he had fallen in love with a snowman with a laugh like an avalanche, but sadly she had still been in love with an English snowman. The Outer Mongolian snowman was too heartbroken to tell Albert any more than that, especially once he realised Albert was the English snowman in question.

And so ten winters went by.

And then twenty winters.

And then fifty.

And then a hundred winters.

Two hundred winters.

Three hundred winters.

Four hundred winters.

Five hundred winters.

Over six hundred winters had passed.

And not once in all that time had Albert and

Clementine's paths ever again crossed.

Despite trying very hard not to cry, Blessing was now openly weeping.

'I really don't know why you are crying so much,' said Albert. 'It didn't happen to you. It happened to me.'

'I'm crying so much because it's the saddest story I've ever heard!' said Blessing.

'Is it really?' asked Albert. 'I thought everybody has a sad story of some kind or other?'

'Most people's sad stories don't last for six hundred winters!' said Blessing.

'Yes, I suppose it has been quite a long time,' agreed Albert. 'That's probably why this winter has been so especially difficult.'

'Wait,' said Blessing. 'Why has this winter been so difficult?'

Albert looked at Blessing as if she had not been listening

to a word he said. In fact, he had simply forgotten to tell her one of the most important parts of the story.

'Because she is here in London,' Albert said. 'Clementine is here.'

Albert had heard it first from Jeremiah, back at the start of December. Of course, he had assumed Jeremiah was talking nonsense because Jeremiah had almost certainly been born in summer. But, after Jeremiah had gone back to his own side of the park, Albert had realised that Jeremiah had been right: Clementine was here!

Ever since Albert had first woken up in London, he had felt peculiar.

Snowmen don't get colds like humans do. Instead, they get warms. Albert had thought he must just have a warm, but snowman warms only ever last for a few days, and Albert had felt peculiar for months now.

So he was not feeling the symptoms of a warm.

He was feeling that Clementine was here, in London.

He could feel it deep down in his most frozen places.

'But if Clementine is here,' interrupted Blessing, 'why wasn't she on the top of the highest hill at midnight on the longest night of the year?'

'She might have been there, I suppose,' said Albert.

'What? What do you mean, she might have been there?' asked Blessing.

'Well, I wouldn't know if she was there or not,' said Albert. 'Because I wasn't there.'

'What?' asked Blessing. 'Why weren't you there?'

'Because I didn't have a disguise,' said Albert. 'So it would have been against the Snowman Code for me to go. Ahem. Ahem.'

'Albert!' said Blessing. 'It was at night-time, and it was important, so it wouldn't have been against the Snowman Code, would it?'

'Well, no,' Albert admitted, 'not strictly speaking.'

'Then why on earth didn't you go?' asked Blessing.

'I suppose I just felt it would have been too sad,' said Albert. 'I have missed her for over six hundred winters, you know.'

'But if you saw her again—'

'If I saw Clementine again, we'd only then have to melt again, and go our separate ways once more. And I don't think I could bear that. Anyway, it has been far too long. Maybe if it had only been three hundred winters I could have gone to meet her. But six hundred winters is – well, it is such a very long time indeed.'

Blessing saw that Albert's bottle-tops had grown glassy, and one of his twig eyebrows was twitching. Sometimes, when Blessing was trying very hard not to cry, her eyebrow twitched too.

'Albert,' she asked, 'have you ever heard the phrase "Better late than never"?'

'Of course I have!' said Albert. 'It has something to do with otters, I believe.'

'It doesn't have anything to do with otters!' said Blessing. 'It means that even if it's late, it's still better to do a thing than never to do it at all.'

'No, I don't think that's right,' said Albert. 'For one thing, I really do think it is to do with otters. For another, I'm perfectly happy here.'

'But if you don't see Clementine you won't ever be ready to melt, and then it will always be winter!' said Blessing.

'But that's all right, you see?' said Albert. 'Nobody is planning to hold a war with Uruguay now. So it's perfectly fine for it to always be winter.'

'It's not perfectly fine for it to always be winter!' said Blessing.

'Do you mean because of the ducks?' asked Albert. 'Because I really wouldn't worry about them. They do complain an awful lot, but, between you and me, I've started to suspect they actually quite enjoy having something to complain about.'

'I don't mean because of the ducks!' said Blessing.

'Oh, then why—' began Albert.

'I already told you why!' interrupted Blessing. 'The winter makes my mum sad, and if it goes on much longer she'll get even sadder and then I'll get sent away again!'

'Right. And is getting sent away really so bad?' asked Albert.

'Yes!' shouted Blessing. 'It really is so bad!'

'But when you really think about it, I mean—' said Albert.

'It's even worse when you really think about it!'

Albert thought about this for a long time, and then sighed.

'Then I suppose you are right,' he said, 'and I had better try to find Clementine. But I should warn you it might take a very long time. I'll have to start by searching all the parks in London. And then, if she isn't in one of the parks, I'll have to look in all the gardens. Do you even know how many gardens there are in London?'

'No,' said Blessing.

'Neither do I,' said Albert. 'But I am sure it is a lot. Maybe as many as seven or eight gardens. So, yes, I will do it. But I should just warn you that it might take years. A lot of years. More even than nine, perhaps.'

'I can't wait nine years for this winter to end!' said Blessing. 'What if I helped you look for Clementine?'

'You can't help me look for her,' said Albert. 'You have to go to school. It's especially important, seeing as you were born in summer.'

'I've missed months of school!' said Blessing. 'Another few weeks while we find Clementine won't make much difference.'

'It would make things go a lot quicker, I suppose,' said Albert.

'Then let's make an ice promise right now that we are going to find Clementine together,' said Blessing.

'This really isn't that kind of thing,' said Albert. 'An ice promise is—'

'Albert Framlington,' Blessing interrupted, 'you ice promise me right now that we will find Clementine together.'

'Fine,' said Albert. 'I ice promise you that we will find Clementine together.'

Blessing saw a faraway look come into Albert's bottle-tops then.

'Are you okay?' she asked, thinking Albert must be feeling very sad about having missed Clementine for over six hundred winters.

'Yes,' replied Albert. 'It's just – I don't suppose finding Clementine is the kind of thing a snowman might be awarded a medal for, is it?'

'Albert, if you find Clementine and stop this endless winter, I ice promise I will award you a medal,' said Blessing.

A delighted smile spread across Albert's face, but it lasted for only a brief moment before his twig eyebrows formed a frown.

'What is it now?' asked Blessing.

'Well, it's just that there are lots of kinds of medals,' explained Albert. 'And many colours of ribbon, so I just want to be sure—'

'A gold medal on a red ribbon,' interrupted Blessing.

'Really?' asked Albert. 'That's what you'll award me? A real gold medal on a real red ribbon?'

'Of course it is,' said Blessing, even though she knew she could not possibly afford to buy Albert a real gold medal. She was not even certain she could afford to buy him a real red ribbon.

'Well, in that case,' said Albert, 'we should get started first thing tomorrow morning!'

'We were going to start then anyway,' said Blessing.

Nine

The next day, Blessing and Albert took the train to Hyde Park to begin their search for Clementine. As they waited on the platform at the station, Blessing asked Albert something she had found herself wondering about: how was it that he could count to six hundred winters or imagine hundreds of roses, but otherwise eight or nine was as high a number as he could even contemplate?

'It's because winters and flowers are so very important,'

Albert said. 'I'd have thought even someone born in summer would have understood that much.'

Luckily, the train pulled into the station then, so Albert did not hear Blessing's reply.

Albert had claimed he had been on plenty of trains before, but as soon as theirs started to move he jumped up on the seat and refused to get down until they reached their destination. Any time the train got too fast for his liking, he would shout, 'Whoa, boy!' and each time it stopped at a station he whispered, 'Giddy up, boy!' until it started moving again. Blessing went and sat in the next carriage but took a seat by the door so she could still keep an eye on him.

Hyde Park was very big, with over three hundred snowmen in residence there. It would have taken weeks to meet all of them, but fortunately the park had its own Snow Mayor. They found him inside his office, an igloo near the boating lake.

The Snow Mayor checked all his records – he did

this just by thinking, because he kept his records in his head – and told them that there was no snowman called Clementine currently living in Hyde Park. But he then added that he had once known a Clementine, fifty winters ago in Berlin. He had been the Snow Mayor of a large park there too and, when all the other snowmen had called a meeting to vote on whether or not to hold a war with the local stray dogs, only this Clementine had spoken out against the idea.

'Yes!' said Albert. 'That's her! That's the snowman we are looking for. How was she?'

'Oh, she was wonderful!' said the Mayor, his two acorn eyes suddenly growing misty at the memory. 'She had a laugh like an avalanche and—'

'Yes, yes, I know that!' interrupted Albert. 'What I really want to know is, did she have a snow husband?'

'Quite the opposite,' said the Snow Mayor. 'She was nursing a broken heart.'

'Oh,' said Albert glumly. 'Then I suppose she must have

had a snow boyfriend the previous winter?'

'Actually, it was the strangest thing,' said the Snow Mayor. 'She told me she had not seen her true love in almost six hundred winters.'

Blessing could not see Albert's bottle-tops from where she was standing. But she was sure that if she could have, they would have looked very glassy indeed.

After all, she could feel her own eyebrows twitching.

Speaking of tears, when Blessing returned home that evening, Margaret was crying.

Adults often cry for more complicated reasons than snowmen or children, and that made it hard to know what to do. If a child is crying, then you might be able to fix it by kissing it better or simply telling them it will all be all right, but those things rarely work so well with an adult. The only thing Blessing knew that ever really helped in this situation was to make her mum a cup of the nice tea

that she liked. It did seem to work a bit, but then later Margaret shut herself in her room and spent a long time talking quietly on the phone. Blessing could not make out what she was saying or who she was talking to, even though she put her ear right up to the door.

Over the next weeks, Blessing and Albert visited more of London's parks.

None of them were large enough to have a Snow Mayor, and so they had to speak to every single snowman individually.

As snowmen are nocturnal, this often meant waking them up. And snowmen are notoriously heavy sleepers, so they can be quite difficult to wake up. And then, once you do manage to wake them up, they are frequently cranky.

So this all took a very long time indeed.

In Green Park, the snowmen spoke with such posh accents it was hard to understand a word they said.

On Clapham Common, Albert got into a shouting match with a Labrador.

In Richmond Park, they were chased by a herd of deer.

In Battersea Park, a snowman who had known Albert in Cairo greeted him like a long-lost brother and insisted they spend the entire afternoon reminiscing about old times. On the way home, Albert complained to Blessing that he had hardly known the snowman. After all, winter in Cairo is only three days long.

Anyway, they carried on, through the parks and green spaces of London.

But they could not find Clementine.

And not one of the snowmen they met could tell them where she was.

Ten

Blessing and Albert had left the most difficult park until last.

Hampstead Heath was so big it was not really a park at all, but more a large piece of countryside marooned in the middle of the city. With over seven hundred snowmen in residence, it should really have had a Snow Mayor, but snowmen living in the countryside are notorious for never being able to agree on anything. When they'd held

their Snow Mayor election at the start of winter, every snowman had voted for himself or herself. To break the deadlock, they had then held a second election, where every snowman was given two votes. Every snowman had simply voted for themself twice.

Blessing and Albert therefore had to walk all over the heath until they had spoken to every single snowman. Each time they passed the frozen ponds, Albert made them stop so that he could once again recount the story of how he had skated there with Clementine in the magical winter of 1773.

It took them nine whole days to talk to every snowman on Hampstead Heath. On the last day, they did so much crisscrossing of the heath that by the time they finished Albert had begun to melt. It was not the kind of melting that could end the entire winter, but it was very much the kind of melting that could cost a snowman an arm or a leg.

Albert explained that he urgently needed to find somewhere nearby that was very cold indeed, so Blessing suggested the penguin enclosure at the zoo. Albert asked

Blessing if she was certain she was born in summer, because that was actually a very good idea.

Fortunately, many animals and humans go into hibernation in winter, so the zoo was quiet. This meant that Albert was able to remove his disguise and enter the penguin enclosure without anybody noticing.

Anybody except the penguins, that is. They certainly noticed! They squawked and flapped their wings at Albert, and they even tried to peck at him until he shooed them away.

Albert later told Blessing that he was surprised the penguins had been so unwelcoming. After all, he had politely introduced himself by telling them that their home country of Africa was one of his favourite places in all the world.

They remained at the zoo until Albert was thoroughly chilled, and then they rode the bus back home in silence.

They had visited every park in London and still they had not found Clementine. That meant she must be in a garden somewhere, so it really might now take them years to find her. And if the winter went on for years, Blessing would definitely get sent away. She might even get sent away more than once!

Still, Article Eight of the Snowman Code says that a snowman always keeps trying.

And so keep trying they did.

Eleven

To help them keep track of their progress through the gardens of London, Blessing borrowed an old book from the bookshelf in their living room at home. It was called *The A to Z of London*, and its pages contained tiny printed maps that showed each and every one of the tens of thousands of streets in the city.

They did not play it very much these days, but Blessing and Margaret had a game where Blessing would pick out a

street from *The A to Z of London,* and ask Margaret if she had ever heard of it. Margaret would reply that never in her whole entire long life had she ever heard of any such place. She would then refuse to believe it was even a real street until Blessing triumphantly showed her it in the A to Z.

Blessing and Margaret would then both agree that London was a very big city indeed, and any person planning to ever get lost in it should always remember to take a copy of *The A to Z of London* with them, otherwise they might never find their way home again. It would then be Margaret's turn to pick out a street, and Blessing's to refuse to believe it was a real street, and so the game would continue.

When Blessing showed Albert Framlington *The A to Z of London,* he laughed and told her there was no need to lug it around with them because he already knew the entire thing by heart. Blessing found this hard to believe. After all, Albert sometimes got lost in Victoria Park, and

Victoria Park was where he lived.

'You're telling me you learned the entire *A to Z of London* by heart?' she asked.

'That's right!' said Albert. 'And not just *The A to Z of London*! *The A to Z of Chicago, The A to Z of Singapore,* The A to Z of the entire United States of Australia, and many more!'

'Then prove it,' said Blessing. 'Tell me everything that is in *The A to Z of London.*'

'Gladly!' said Albert. 'The first letter in *The A to Z of London* is A, for aardvark. Next is B, which is for balloon. Then C is for seaside. And then after that it just goes something, something, something until Z is for zebra. You see! I told you I knew the entire A to Z of London by heart.'

Blessing stared at Albert.

'Oh, I know what you are thinking,' said Albert. 'You are thinking, "How could one single snowman possibly remember all the letters in the A to Z of so many different

places?" Well, I'll let you into a secret.' Albert moved closer and lowered his voice. 'Just between you and me, it's the same A to Z for anywhere that speaks English! It starts with aardvark and ends with zebra every single time!'

'That's not the A to Z,' said Blessing. 'That's the alphabet.'

'Yes, and that's exactly the same thing!' said Albert. 'The A to Z is the alphabet!'

'It's not the same thing at all,' said Blessing. 'The alphabet is a list of all the letters in a language. *The A to Z of London* is this book. It contains every street in London.'

Albert studied the cover of the small book and knitted his twig eyebrows into a frown.

'You're telling me that little book contains every street in London?'

'Yes!' said Blessing.

'I don't think that's even possible,' said Albert. 'I mean, how would they fit them all in? And what about the people that live on those streets? I can't imagine they would be

very happy to come home and find that their street has been squished up inside that little book.'

'It doesn't contain the actual streets, Albert!' said Blessing. 'It's a book of maps. See?'

Blessing opened the A to Z and flicked through its pages. As Albert looked at them, Blessing saw a small amount of steam emerge from the place where his ears would have been.

'Are you all right, Albert?' she asked. 'Because I don't want to alarm you, but you have steam coming out—'

'I'm better than all right!' interrupted Albert. 'Releasing a little steam from the place where our ears would be is what snowmen do when we've had a brilliant idea! Thinking up something very clever tends to overheat our snow brains a little, you see.'

'And have you had a brilliant idea?' asked Blessing.

'Yes,' said Albert. 'I have! I think it is one of my best ideas ever.'

'So what is it?' asked Blessing.

'This alphabet book of yours, do you know what we should do? We should bring it with us, and we can use it to keep track of all the streets we have visited!'

Blessing found herself staring at Albert in disbelief again.

'What do you think?' he asked her. 'About my idea, I mean?'

'I think it's an excellent idea,' said Blessing. 'And whoever thought of it should be very proud of themselves.'

'Exactly!' agreed Albert. 'I am!'

Twelve

Blessing and Albert quickly discovered that if they split up, they could cover a page of the A to Z each day. So every morning they took the bus to a new page, and on the way there they carefully divided its streets and gardens between them. Blessing was always given more streets and gardens to explore. Albert explained this was because he was older, and everybody knew that older people were supposed to do less work. Sometimes he even claimed this was in the

Snowman Code, but anytime Blessing asked which Article it was, Albert quickly changed the subject.

At lunchtime, Blessing would always find Albert asleep in one of his assigned gardens. She would shake him awake and remind him that he should have been looking for Clementine. Albert would ignore this and ask what was for lunch, even though snowmen do not even need to eat lunch.

They would then repeat the process in the afternoon, Blessing scoring off her last streets by the light of the streetlamps until she once again located Albert asleep under a hedge or behind a shed.

On the bus home, Albert would ask Blessing if they had completed another entire page of the A to Z that day. Blessing would confirm that they had, but would also point out that Albert had spent much of the day asleep. Albert would only ever nod approvingly and tell Blessing that this was exactly what was meant by the saying, 'Teamwork makes the dream work.'

Yet even though Blessing worked so hard, and Albert worked so sort-of hard, it was not enough. *The A to Z of London* was over five hundred pages long. And by the middle of May, they had only completed thirty-four of those pages. At this rate, it might take them two years to find Clementine.

Meantime, it was still the depths of winter, and Blessing's mum was not getting any happier. In fact, Margaret was getting only sadder. She was so sad that on some days now she would even still be in bed when Blessing got home.

Then, just before lunchtime on the thirty-fifth day of their search, a snowman in a garden in Crouch End asked Blessing why in the name of Gurk was she looking for a snowman during the daytime anyway.

'What do you mean?' asked Blessing.

'We snowmen are famously nocturnal,' yawned the snowman. 'So, if I wanted to find one snowman in particular, I wouldn't go around bothering snowmen in the privacy of their own gardens when they are trying to get

a peaceful day's sleep. No, I'd look in the place we all go in the middle of the night.'

'Which is where?' asked Blessing.

'The Flower Market,' said the snowman.

'The Flower Market?'

'That's right,' explained the sleepy snowman. 'You see, wherever we are it's always winter, so the Flower Market is the only place we ever get to see flowers.'

Blessing recalled the faraway look in Albert's bottle-tops as he had imagined the Rose Garden in summer. 'And do all snowmen like flowers?' she asked.

The snowman looked at Blessing like she had been born at noon on midsummer's day.

'Do all snowmen like flowers? We love them! And they love us just as much, because we are the world's number one pollinators of flowers. Without snowmen, there wouldn't even be any flowers!'

'You're thinking of bees,' said Blessing.

'Nope,' said the snowman. 'Definitely snowmen.'

By now, Blessing knew that there was little point arguing with a snowman who believed he was right. To a snowman, believing he was right and being right were exactly the same thing.

'Well, do you think Clementine – the snowman I'm looking for – will be at the Flower Market tonight?' asked Blessing.

'Oh, we don't all go every night, of course. But most of us do try and get along there at least once a week. It's good for our spirits, you see,' said the snowman.

'Thank you for telling me about this,' said Blessing.

'I really didn't have a choice,' yawned the snowman. 'The Snowman Code says we must always help a child in need.'

'Yes,' said Blessing. 'It does say that, doesn't it?'

Blessing found Albert asleep inside a wheelbarrow and tipped him out into the snow.

'What did you do that for?' he said crossly. 'I wasn't asleep if that's what you thought. I was just resting with my eyes closed, and also having a dream at the same time. Nothing wrong with that at all.'

'Why didn't you tell me we might be able to find Clementine at the Flower Market?' asked Blessing.

'The Flower Market?' said Albert. 'Well, yes, I suppose that could be an idea. Ahem.'

Blessing saw that Albert had turned red.

'Albert! Why didn't you tell me we could look for her there?'

'I didn't think to.' Albert shrugged. 'Ahem. Anyway, come along – if we don't hurry up, we won't finish our page of the alphabet today.'

And with that Albert stood up, dusted himself off and began looking in gardens more enthusiastically than he had done in weeks.

Thirteen

Late that night, Blessing waited until Margaret was asleep.

And then she waited another hour, just to be sure.

And then one more hour, just to be really sure.

And then she snuck outside.

The streets were empty. After all, it was long past midnight. And, even though it was May, it was still the depths of winter.

Another child might have been scared to be out

past midnight in empty streets in the depths of winter.

Blessing, of course, was not the kind of child to be scared of anything.

So she hurried to the park, climbed over the gate, jumped down into the snow on the other side with a **crunch** and then **crunch-slurped** her way through the park.

When Blessing reached Albert, he was fast asleep.

'I thought you were supposed to be nocturnal!' she said.

'I am!' said Albert, waking up with a start. 'But being nocturnal doesn't mean I stay wide awake all night.'

'That's exactly what it means,' said Blessing.

'Well, what are you doing here, anyway?' asked Albert. 'You're not supposed to be nocturnal. You're not even a marsupial.'

'I'm here because we're going to the Flower Market,' said Blessing.

'My sweet summer child!' laughed Albert. 'We can't possibly go to the Flower Market. It's very late at night

now, and the Flower Market opens very early in the morning.'

'Very late at night and very early in the morning are the same thing!' said Blessing.

Albert's twig eyebrows knitted themselves into a frown. 'Are you quite sure about that?' he asked. 'That doesn't sound at all right to me.'

'I'm completely sure!' said Blessing.

'In that case, we'd better get going,' said Albert. 'Come along.'

'Do you know the way?' asked Blessing.

'Do I know the way to the Flower Market? Of course I do!' said Albert. 'I'm a snowman!'

Albert did not know the way to the Flower Market.

They got so lost that even the A to Z could not help them, and they ended up having to take a taxi. The taxi driver asked Blessing what such a young girl was doing

out at this time of night. Blessing told her that she was going on a very special class trip to the Flower Market. It was not as good a cover story as a kangaroo sanctuary in Australia, but it was the best Blessing could do at such short notice.

When they arrived, the Flower Market looked like a surprisingly ordinary sort of market. There were perhaps a dozen flower stalls, and lots of men and women working. They wore hats and gloves and scarves against the cold, and they all seemed very busy.

They were loading and unloading flowers.

Counting them and weighing them.

Wrapping them and unwrapping them.

Arranging them by type and colour and length.

'Oh, isn't it marvellous?' declared Albert. 'Isn't the Flower Market just the most wonderful place there is?'

'But where are all the snowmen and—'

Blessing stopped talking then because she had seen that Albert had removed his hat and sunglasses. The Flower Market workers had seen this too. They had all stopped what they were doing and were staring at Albert.

'Albert!' whispered Blessing. 'What are you doing? They can see you're a snowman!'

But Albert had now begun to wave his hat at the workers. 'Good evening!' he shouted. 'Good evening, human workers of the Flower Market!'

'Good evening, Mr Snowman!' they shouted back, then returned to their work as if they were quite used to being greeted by a snowman in the middle of the night.

Blessing stared at Albert, and then at the workers, and then back at Albert.

For the very first time in her ten-and-a-half winters and summers, Blessing found herself completely and utterly speechless.

A market worker standing nearby now pointed to a large door.

'You two can go right on in,' she said.

Albert opened the door for Blessing.

'Come along,' he said.

'Yes,' said Blessing, her voice beginning to return to her, 'I'm coming.'

As soon as Blessing was inside, she found herself completely and utterly speechless for the very second time in her ten-and-a-half winters and summers.

Because that outside part had merely been the entrance. The real Flower Market was in here. And there were ten times as many stalls and a hundred times as many flowers as there had been outside.

There were vast piles of pink carnations.

And huge bundles of blue roses.

And great mounds of white lilies.

And giant stacks of yellow daffodils.

And entire pyramids of red snapdragons.

There were so many flowers that inside the Flower Market it was just like spring or summer!

Well, it was just like spring or summer except for two things.

The first was that the Flower Market was colder even than the winter night outside.

And the second was that it was full of snowmen.

There must have been hundreds of them. Hundreds of snowmen—

Arranging flowers.

Posing with flowers.

Smelling flowers.

Tickling each other with flowers.

Fainting from the excitement of smelling and being tickled with so many delicious flowers.

Then having to be revived with ice and the smell of other delicious flowers!

Blessing did not faint, but it did take her quite some time to get her voice back.

'Don't the market workers mind all these snowmen being here?' she eventually asked, once she was able to speak again.

'Mind?' asked Albert. 'Of course they don't mind! They love having us here! Us snowmen are famous for being able to cool a room right down. We keep the flowers so fresh and beautiful. And it's a good chilly cold that we provide. Far better than any refrigerator.'

'I suppose that makes sense,' said Blessing. 'Sort of.'

'Now, what kind of flowers shall we smell first?' asked Albert. 'Those geraniums over there look nice. But I don't mind telling you that if we could only find some lovely tulips—'

'Albert!' said Blessing. 'We're not here to smell flowers. We're here to find Clementine!'

'Right. Yes. Well, I can't see her.' Albert shrugged. 'Can you?'

'We don't even know what she looks like!' said Blessing.

'Exactly. So no point wasting time with that,' said Albert. 'Now, about those tulips—'

'Albert!' said Blessing again. 'We aren't here to look for tulips. We're here to look for Clementine! And we're going to ask every single one of these snowmen if they've seen her!'

'Yes. That's it!' said Albert. 'That's it exactly. We'll ask them if they have seen Clementine. And, while we are talking to them, we can also ask them if they happen to have seen any nice tulips. I mean, it can't possibly hurt, can it?'

An hour later, Blessing had spoken to every snowman in the Flower Market. Albert claimed he had spoken to many of them too, but the pollen covering his potato nose and snowy chin told a different story. It did not matter though, because none of the snowmen had seen Clementine. None of them had ever even heard her name, or her laugh like an avalanche.

And yet it had still been a successful outing. In one

single hour, Blessing had spoken to an entire week's worth of snowmen, and none of them had even needed to be woken up. On the night bus home, Blessing told Albert that if they kept coming to the Flower Market, she was sure they would encounter Clementine soon enough.

'Yes,' agreed Albert dreamily. 'They really did smell delicious. And what colours! Mmm, those chrysanthemums.'

Back at home, Blessing crept up into her room and climbed into bed.

When her alarm went off, she was so tired she felt as if she had only been asleep for an hour.

And the reason for that was that she had in fact only been asleep for an hour.

Fourteen

That next day was a Wednesday.

Blessing had never liked Wednesdays. The thing about Wednesday was the way that it put itself right there in the middle of the week. It was as if Wednesday had something to hide.

And the thing about that was, Wednesday often did have something to hide. Tuesday might have been the day when things most liked to change, but if things went badly

wrong, they usually went badly wrong on a Wednesday.

And today was one such Wednesday.

The first clue was the phone ringing very early in the morning, and Blessing's mum taking it into her room and closing the door.

Then, right as Blessing was leaving to pretend to go to school, the doorbell rang. It was Jasmine, and she had a policewoman with her.

'Yes, that's her,' Blessing told the policewoman. 'I'd recognise her anywhere. Take her away, lock her up and throw away the key!'

'Hi, Blessing,' said Jasmine. 'Can we come in, please?'

'No,' said Blessing. 'And if I don't invite you in, you can't come in.'

'Actually, we can,' said the policewoman.

'Maybe you can,' Blessing said to the policewoman. 'But she can't.'

'What? Why can't I come in?' asked Jasmine.

'Your kind can't go anywhere if they're not invited in,' said Blessing.

'What do you mean, "your kind"?' asked Jasmine. 'Do you mean social workers?'

'I mean vampires,' explained Blessing.

Jasmine and the policewoman laughed then, as if Blessing had just made a hilarious joke.

But Blessing had not been making a joke.

And anyway Jasmine and the policewoman had not come to hear jokes.

They had come to take Margaret to hospital.

And to send Blessing away.

Blessing ducked under the legs of the policewoman and ran out of the house.

Soon she was running down the street, then across the bridge over the duck pond and then over the pitches to the

place where Albert lived. As she got close, she saw that Jeremiah was beside him.

'Albert!' she said. 'Put your disguise on! We have to find Clementine right now!'

'Ahem,' said Albert.

'I mean it!' said Blessing. 'There's no more time! We have to find her right now!'

'You do say some very funny things,' said Jeremiah. 'Were you born in summer?'

'She was, you know,' said Albert.

'What do you mean by that, Jeremiah?' asked Blessing.

'Well, saying that you have to find Clementine—' said Jeremiah.

'But we do have to find her!' said Blessing. 'They're taking my mum to hospital!'

'Oh dear,' said Jeremiah. 'It's her appendix, isn't it? Such dreadful things.'

'It's not her appendix!' said Blessing. 'It's because she's sad because this winter has gone on too long, which is why

we have to find Clementine and end it right now!'

'That does all sound very serious,' said Jeremiah. 'But I still don't really see how you can find Clementine when we already know exactly where she is.'

'Ahem,' Albert coughed. 'Ahem.'

'What do you mean, we already know where Clementine is?' asked Blessing. 'Who already knows where she is?'

'We do!' said Jeremiah. 'She is in front of the Town Hall. Next to the big Christmas tree. She has been there all winter. As soon as I saw her there back in December, I immediately came and told Albert.'

Albert had turned bright red. 'I don't think you did tell me that, Jeremiah. And if you did I must have forgotten. And she's probably not even still there anyway, so—'

'No, she is still there,' interrupted Jeremiah. 'I saw her yesterday. I just told you that.'

Blessing stared at Albert.

'You knew where Clementine was all along? You knew it the whole time we were searching all those parks and

gardens?' she asked him. 'How could you do that to me, Albert?'

And then they heard a siren.

A police car was driving across the pitches towards them.

This time, Blessing did not even bother trying to run away. She just stood there, staring at Albert. And when the policewoman opened the door of the car, she went across and got in without even having to be asked.

Fifteen

There were many things that were right about Miriam and John's house.

Miriam and John were very nice people.

They lived just on the other side of the park.

They gave Blessing her own room, and the bed in it was very comfortable.

They had a big television and an excellent selection of biscuits.

They had a well-stocked art cupboard, and Blessing was allowed to use whatever she liked from it.

They even had a friendly dog. His name was Nelson, and he had outlandishly large paws.

In fact, there was only one thing wrong with Miriam and John's house. But this one thing meant everything. Because the one thing wrong with Miriam and John's house was that it was not home.

Home was where Blessing's own bed was.

It was where all her favourite things were.

Her books, her chemistry set, her own art supplies and her window that looked out on so many other people's back windows it was like having a giant television with a hundred channels you could watch all at once.

Most of all, home was where her mum was.

Blessing lay down on the large and comfortable bed and cried.

Nelson jumped up and placed both his outlandishly large paws on her.

It made her feel a bit better.

But still.

It was not home.

And not even a kindly dog with outlandishly large paws could make it home.

At breakfast the next day, Miriam offered to walk Blessing to school.

Blessing said she could manage herself, but Miriam said she felt like a walk, anyway.

That meant Miriam knew Blessing had not been going to school.

And that meant that Jasmine knew too.

And that meant that Miss Hazelworst knew Blessing was not living in a kangaroo sanctuary in the outback of Australia after all.

Things were even worse than Blessing had realised.

Their walk took them through Victoria Park and around the edge of the pitches.

When Blessing glanced over at Albert, he was staring right at her. And even though it was completely against the Snowman Code, Albert actually waved at Blessing when Miriam was not looking.

Blessing did not wave back.

School was bad, but not as bad as it could have been. Nobody mentioned kangaroos or Australia or even asked Blessing where she had been for so many months. In fact, the only people who spoke to her about anything at all that had happened since the last time she had been at school were the Driplet Triplets.

'Please don't ever set the Abominable Snowman on us

again,' whispered Ashby Tregdahornick.

'We're all very sorry,' mumbled Cynthia Smith-Smith.

'Very sorry,' murmured Bartholomew Weaselton.

After school, Blessing walked back along the far edge of the pitches, as far from Albert as she could possibly get. But she trod as loudly as she could, so that Albert could hear every crunch-slurp. After all, Albert Framlington and his astonishing selfishness were responsible for every single crunch-slurp of this never-ending winter.

Albert Framlington and his astonishing selfishness had ruined everything.

The next morning, Miriam allowed Blessing to walk to school by herself.

Albert had moved himself to the side of the pitches that

Blessing had walked along yesterday, so she now walked along the opposite side.

By home time, Albert had repositioned himself on that opposite side, so Blessing returned to her original route.

Even from a distance, she could tell that Albert had been crying, because tiny icicles had formed beneath his bottle-tops, and they glinted in the cold winter sun.

'Good,' Blessing said to herself. 'He should cry. He caused this endless winter, and he got my mum sent away, and he ruined everything!'

Sixteen

A few days later, Miriam took Blessing to visit her mum in hospital.

It was not like any hospital Blessing had ever been to before. The patients all had their own bedrooms, and there did not seem to be any doctors or nurses. Miriam had to explain that the doctors and nurses did not wear uniforms here. Blessing wondered how anybody was supposed to get better if nobody even knew who were

the patients and who were the staff.

When they got to her mum's bedroom, Blessing could tell right away that coming into hospital had not made Margaret any happier. In fact, it seemed to have only made her worse. Margaret even spoke and moved more slowly now, as if being very sad could weaken your muscles and bones.

They sat in glum silence for a few minutes, and then Miriam suggested they go outside and explore the grounds. They all agreed this was an excellent idea, but when they got outside Margaret burst into tears as soon as she saw the snow that still blanketed everything.

So they went to the cafeteria instead, and Blessing told her mum it would be spring soon. Any day now, Margaret would wake up, see the green grass outside, and feel so much better that she'd be able to come home immediately. Miriam frowned and said that the people on television thought there might not be a spring at all this year, because the weather really was very broken indeed. Some people

even thought it might just be winter forever now.

Margaret had seemed like she might cry again then, and so that was when Blessing told them.

She told them everything.

She told them that snowmen were all alive.

And that if you talked to them six times the Snowman Code meant that they had to answer you.

And that even though the weather was broken now it was not the reason it was still winter.

The reason it was still winter was because winter only ended when all the snowmen in a place were ready to melt.

And there was this one snowman called Albert Framlington.

And he had once been in love with this other snowman called Clementine.

But then they had melted to prevent a war being held with Uruguay.

And Albert had missed Clementine for over six hundred winters.

But now they were both here in London, and Albert was too scared to talk to Clementine.

But when he did so he would be ready to melt.

And then winter would finally end and spring would come.

And then Margaret would immediately feel better and she and Blessing could both go home.

A woman sitting near them in the cafeteria had been listening to what Blessing said with increasing interest.

When Blessing finished speaking, she introduced herself as Margaret's doctor and asked if she could have a chat with Blessing. Miriam said that she thought that would be a very good idea.

The doctor took Blessing into a small office and told her that she knew things were difficult, but it was important for Blessing to be realistic and not to make up silly stories. She said there were no talking snowmen, and anyway Margaret was now so sad that she might not even notice the end of winter when it came.

Blessing could feel herself starting to tear up. She tried to hide it, but the doctor must have noticed, because the tone of her voice changed then. She explained that the reason she was telling Blessing all this was only because she did not want Blessing to be very disappointed when spring arrived and Margaret did not get better. For some reason, it seemed important to the doctor that Blessing was very disappointed as soon as possible.

Afterwards, the doctor walked Blessing back to the

cafeteria. As they all said their goodbyes, the doctor told Miriam and Blessing it was good that they had come today, because it gave them a chance to wish Margaret a happy birthday.

Her mum's birthday!

It was the day after tomorrow!

How could Blessing have forgotten?

They had to come back to the hospital then!

Miriam said she would be happy to bring Blessing back if the doctor said it was okay. But the doctor said that today's visit had already been quite enough excitement for Margaret for one week.

At Miriam and John's that night, Blessing ate her dinner in silence.

Miriam asked if she was upset about missing her mum's birthday, but Blessing shook her head. Miriam said that Blessing could always talk to her, but Blessing could not

talk to her. After all, she was not only upset about missing her mum's birthday. She was also upset about having to stay at Miriam and John's house.

So Blessing waited until she was in bed that night to cry, and then cried quietly enough that nobody would hear her.

Well, almost nobody.

Fortunately, dogs have excellent hearing, so Nelson heard and jumped up and put his outlandishly large paws around Blessing in a kind of canine cuddle.

Thank goodness for dogs!

Seventeen

Thump!

In the small hours of the morning, Blessing and Nelson awoke with a start.

If humans and dogs were able to talk to one another, they would have asked each other the very same question: 'What on earth was that?'

Thump!

There it was again.

It sounded like an owl had flown into the bedroom window.

But owls are clever birds, so they do not generally fly into bedroom windows.

And they certainly do not do so twice.

Thump!

There it was a third time.

And in the entire history of owls, no owl has ever flown into a bedroom window three times in quick succession.

Another child and another dog might have been scared to peek out and discover what kind of creature had thumped three times on their bedroom window in the small hours of the night. But this is Blessing and Nelson we are talking about here, so instead of hiding under the covers they both now got up and hurried over to the window.

And it turned out there was nothing whatsoever to be scared of.

Because Albert Framlington was standing in the garden, throwing snowballs at the window.

In fact, he had just launched another one.

Thump!

Nelson started barking, because after all dogs dislike snowmen just as much as snowmen dislike dogs, and here was a snowman standing in Nelson's very own garden throwing snowballs at Nelson's very own house.

'Shhhh, Nelson! He's not a bad snowman,' Blessing said, then corrected herself. 'Well, he is. But I know him.'

Down in the garden, Albert was preparing yet another snowball. Blessing hurriedly opened the window.

'Stop that!' she hissed. 'You'll wake Miriam and John. And why aren't you wearing your disguise? You're breaking the Snowman Code!'

'I'm not breaking the Snowman Code,' Albert said, 'because it's after midnight and this is very important! Can we come in, please?'

'What do you mean, "we"?' asked Blessing.

Jeremiah now stepped out from the bushes and raised his deerstalker hat in greeting.

'Good evening, Blessing.'

'Hi, Jeremiah.'

Nelson began barking again. One snowman in his very own garden is a lot to ask any dog to put up with, but two – well, two is too much.

'Can we come in, please?' asked Albert.

'Just you, Albert,' said Blessing. 'Sorry, Jeremiah.'

'I quite understand,' called Jeremiah. 'Anyway, I have my pipe to entertain myself with.'

'It's not a real pipe,' said Albert.

'Shhhh!' said Blessing. 'Come to the back door.'

And so, in the small hours of the morning, Albert and Blessing sat round Miriam and John's kitchen table. Nelson positioned himself in the corner, staring at Albert and growling every time he moved.

'So, what do you want?' asked Blessing.

'I have broken the Snowman Code,' sighed Albert,

'because I could have helped you and I didn't. I'm ever so sorry, and I want to make it up to you by helping you now.'

'Are you just saying that because you want a medal?' asked Blessing.

'No,' said Albert sadly. 'I don't deserve to be awarded a medal after what I've done. Not even a silver one on a blue ribbon.'

'Well, you're too late to help now, anyway. My mum is in hospital.'

'Icebergs!' said Albert. 'Appendixes really are such terrible things.'

'Albert! How many times? It's not her appendix!' said Blessing. 'It's that this endless winter has made her so sad. The doctor says she's so sad that even spring coming might not make her happy now.'

'That doesn't sound right to me,' said Albert. 'Was this doctor born in summer?'

'No,' said Blessing, suddenly feeling very sad herself. 'I don't think she was.'

'Well, I'm going to try to help you, anyway,' said Albert. 'After all, better late than never.'

Blessing looked at Albert.

'I don't mean about otters, if that's what you're thinking,' he said. 'I mean that I'm going to melt for you. But I can't do that until I see Clementine. And I'm scared to see her. So, the thing is, I need you to come with me.'

'Why?' asked Blessing.

'Because you're my friend. And so I think, if you were with me, I wouldn't be quite so scared.'

'Maybe you should take Jeremiah,' said Blessing. 'He's the one who knows where Clementine is.'

'Jeremiah was born in summer,' said Albert.

'So was I,' said Blessing.

'Not like Jeremiah was,' said Albert. 'I need your help to do this, Blessing. Will you come with me?'

'Yes,' said Blessing. 'Of course I will.'

It would have been a tender moment between the two old friends, but right then Nelson decided that he could

not stand having this snowman in his very own kitchen any longer. He let out a loud howl, and then he started barking, and would not be shushed until Blessing had bustled Albert Framlington out of the back door.

'Come tomorrow night,' she told him. 'I'll be ready.'

Eighteen

Thump!

The snowball arrived in the small hours of the next morning.

Blessing – who had gone to bed wearing all her clothes – crept downstairs and went outside. But as soon as she closed the back door Nelson started barking. He barked so loudly that she had to open the door and let him come with them.

Nelson barked once at Albert Framlington, twice at Jeremiah, and then fell into step alongside Blessing. Dogs do not like snowmen, but they do very much like adventures. They like adventures so much, they are even willing to put up with a snowman or two if it means they get to go on one.

The Town Hall was on the High Street, which was back on the other side of the park. When they got to the park gate, Albert lifted Nelson over and passed him to Jeremiah. As soon as he was safely back on the snowy ground, Nelson yelped in puzzlement.

They made their way across the pitches, towards the duck pond.

They crossed the bridge, and looked down and saw beneath them that the ducks were all fast asleep, their beaks tucked into their feathers to keep them warm.

They followed the path past the Rose Garden and took

the lane that leads to the canal.

They walked along the towpath, past all the canal boats that had been frozen in place for so many months.

As they passed the big houses that backed on to the canal, a light suddenly came on in a kitchen. They all froze as a man in his pyjamas came to the window and stared directly at them as he drank a glass of water. He then shook his head, turned out the light and headed back upstairs. In the morning, he would tell his wife that he had seen two snowmen, a girl and a dog with outlandishly large paws walking along the towpath. She would tell him that he really must stop eating cheese before going to bed.

From the towpath, they took an alley that brought them out on to the High Street, and from there they could already see the Town Hall. In front of it was a Christmas tree, which was still standing in May because the Mayor had insisted that if there was still going to be snow then there must still be a Christmas tree too.

And there, just beyond the Christmas tree – and exactly

where Jeremiah had said she would be – was Clementine.

She had mismatched marbles for eyes, a button for a nose and her smile was a slightly crooked stick.

She looked just like any other snowman, but of course that was the whole point.

Because Albert had not fallen in love with the parsnip of Clementine's nose or the coal of her eyes or even the tartan of her scarf, for all those things were just temporary decorations. He had fallen in love with her heart and her laugh like an avalanche.

And the way he looked at her now, it was clear that his feelings had not changed in over six hundred winters.

So Albert stared at Clementine.

And Blessing and Jeremiah and Nelson all stared at Albert.

None of them had ever seen a look of such love before.

Jeremiah even removed his pipe from his mouth.

And then, after some time, Albert began to walk towards Clementine. Jeremiah moved to go with him, but

Blessing held him back and even Nelson growled at him.

Clementine did not hear Albert approaching until he was very close. And then she turned round and saw him, and when she did she froze.

And Albert Framlington froze too.

And the two of them stared at each other for a very long time.

And then Clementine stepped forward and hugged Albert.

And Albert hugged her back.

And then they spoke for only a few brief moments.

And then Albert turned and walked back to the others.

The two snowmen, one girl and one dog with outlandishly large paws silently retraced their steps, down the High Street, through the alley, along the towpath, up the lane, through the park and over the gate. They were back at Miriam and John's house before any of them spoke again.

'Well,' asked Jeremiah. 'What happened?'

'Nothing, really.' Albert shrugged.

'Nothing, really?' asked Blessing. 'You see Clementine for the first time in six hundred winters and nothing really happens?'

'That's right,' said Albert.

'But what did you say to each other?' asked Blessing.

'I just told her that I had missed her and I had always loved her and she told me the exact same thing,' said Albert. 'But we're going to try and see each other tomorrow. And

I think it might be a few more days before we are ready to melt. I hope that's all right?'

'Of course that's all right,' said Blessing.

'Fine by me too,' said Jeremiah. 'Gives me time to say a proper farewell to this pipe of mine.'

'I wasn't asking you,' said Albert.

Nineteen

The next day, Blessing decided not to go to school.

This time, it wasn't because of the Driplet Triplets. It was because she was too sad. Today was her mum's birthday, and what sort of a world is it when you cannot even see your mum on her birthday?

It was all a bit much.

So Blessing went to the museum with the giant walrus and his freshly polished tusks, and then she snuck into

the theatre, right under the nose of the usher who had told her she might be sent to prison. And when neither of those things made her even the slightest bit happy, she went to the cinema. The movie did not get off to a good start, because one of the two lead characters looked like Jasmine, and the other one looked a lot like the doctor who had wanted Blessing to be disappointed as soon as possible.

But ten minutes into the movie, a curious thing happened. An odd-looking couple bundled up in hats, scarves, coats and sunglasses entered the cinema and sat in the very front row. There was something about them that seemed – well, not quite right. It took Blessing longer than it probably should have to realise that the thing that was not quite right about these people was that they were snowmen. And not just any old snowmen, but Albert and Clementine.

But Blessing did not go over and say hello to them.

Nor did she continue to watch the movie.

Instead, Blessing sat in the cinema and watched Albert

and Clementine watch the movie.

Blessing could tell that Clementine had never seen a movie before because she kept shouting out to the actors as if they could hear her. But the strange thing was that Albert was shouting out to the actors too. Blessing had already explained to Albert what an actor was, and he had insisted he knew fine well what an actor was, because he used to be a Hollywood snowman.

It was all very curious. After all, for as long as Blessing had known him, Albert Framlington had seemed every one of his six hundred winters. Yet here he was now, behaving as if he had been born just a few summers ago!

But Albert acting so oddly was not the only strange thing that happened that afternoon. Because seeing Albert and Clementine having so much fun together made Blessing feel something she realised she had not felt in a long time now.

It made her feel happy.

And right as Blessing realised that, something up on the

screen made Clementine laugh, and her laugh really did sound just like an avalanche. And the sound of Clementine laughing like an avalanche made Blessing even happier still.

But perhaps that should not be surprising. After all, an avalanche is something very powerful that can sweep you up and carry you along with it. So it makes sense that exactly the same thing is true of a laugh like an avalanche.

Twenty

Lying in her bed at Miriam and John's that night, Blessing had a brilliant idea.

It was such a brilliant idea that if Blessing had been a snowman, steam would have come out of the place where her ears would have been. But as Blessing was not a snowman, she instead simply whispered, 'Yes!'

Nelson looked at her and tilted his head to the left.

Blessing spoke just enough Dog to know that in Nelson's language this meant, 'What?'

And so Blessing explained her brilliant idea to Nelson.

It went like this.

Albert and Clementine had lost touch after they had melted at the end of the Great Winter of 1773. And the reason Albert had been too scared to see Clementine this winter was because he could not stand the thought of losing her all over again the next time they melted. But there was a way that two snowmen could always find each other every time they melted, no matter where in the world they next woke up.

They could keep in contact through a human!

As soon as they awoke in a new place, Albert and Clementine could each send Blessing a postcard. And Blessing could look at the map in the school library, and work out if one of them should travel to the other, or if they should meet in the middle. For instance, if one snowman was in New Zealand, and the other was in San Francisco,

then she could tell them to meet in Japan!

And if meeting that winter was impractical, Blessing could help them exchange letters until the next winter.

It was completely foolproof! Even Nelson seemed about to bark his approval when—

Thump!

Blessing and Nelson crept to the window and looked out. Albert, Jeremiah and Clementine were all standing in Miriam and John's garden. They were waving at Blessing to come down.

This time, Nelson did not even bark at them. And that is quite something when you consider how dogs generally feel about snowmen.

When they got out into the garden, Clementine stepped forward to hug Blessing.

'It's such a pleasure to meet you,' she said. 'I've heard so much about you.'

'I've heard so much about you too,' said Blessing. 'But why are you all here?'

'Take a deep breath and tell me what you can smell,' said Albert.

'Apart from my pipe, of course,' added Jeremiah.

'For the ninth time,' said Albert, 'she can't smell your pipe, because there is no tobacco in it, because it's not a real pipe.'

Blessing took a deep breath in.

'You see?' Jeremiah said proudly. 'Tobacco.'

'I don't smell tobacco, Jeremiah,' said Blessing. 'But I do smell—'

And then she stopped.

Blessing knew exactly what she could smell.

She did not want to believe it.

For lots of reasons.

And yet there it was.

It was undeniable.

And now Nelson sniffed the air too, and then ran around in delighted circles, chasing his tail.

Because even though there was still the snow on the ground.

And the night was cold and dark as midwinter.

And the air was crisp and clear as a church bell in the distance.

The smell was unmistakable.

It was the smell of spring.

Feeling her eyes start to well up, Blessing quickly wiped away the gathering tears.

'Are you crying?' asked Albert. 'I thought you'd be pleased.'

'I am pleased,' said Blessing. 'I just don't want to have to say goodbye to you all.'

'We still have some time together yet!' said Albert. 'Do you remember what Article Nine of the Snowman Code says we must do now?'

'No,' said Blessing. 'I don't think I do.'

'It says we must have a great big party to celebrate the coming of spring!' said Jeremiah.

'That sounds nice,' said Blessing. 'I hope you all have a lovely time.'

'Blessing! You have to come to the party with us!' said Clementine. 'That's why we're here.'

But Blessing did not feel she could celebrate the coming of spring. Not when it meant she might never see them again.

'I'm sorry,' she said. 'I just don't know if I really feel like going to a party right now.'

'But when you don't feel like going to a party,' said Clementine, 'why, that is the perfect time to go to a party!'

'Is it?' Blessing asked.

'Of course!' said Albert. 'Because that is exactly when you are in most need of a party. And, by the way, we all think you should bring a special guest too.'

'What?' asked Blessing. 'Who would I bring?'

'You know somebody else who needs a party too, don't you?' asked Clementine.

'My mum,' said Blessing. 'But they wouldn't let her out

of the hospital. And, even if they did, how would we even get her to a party?'

'We'd take her in our ambulance, of course!' said Jeremiah.

Blessing waited for Albert to say something about Jeremiah having been born in summer, but he did not. Instead, he stepped slightly to the side, so that Blessing could see out into the street where an ambulance was parked.

'Where did you get that?' asked Blessing.

'I have a friend who is a snowman outside a hospital in Bermondsey,' said Clementine.

'And can you drive it?' asked Blessing.

'I can!' Jeremiah said proudly. 'One winter I was a snowman at a driving school in Korea. So I am an excellent driver!'

'Except you sometimes forget you aren't still in Korea, and end up driving on the wrong side of the road,' said Clementine.

'Yes, I do sometimes do that,' agreed Jeremiah. 'But it's all part of the adventure.'

Nelson, who spoke just enough human to recognise the word 'adventure', barked.

Twenty-one

All things considered, it was surprisingly easy to kidnap Margaret from the hospital.

It probably helped that none of the nurses or doctors wore uniforms. After all, that meant that when Albert and Clementine arrived wearing the uniforms they had found in the ambulance, they looked very official indeed. The duty nurse was so impressed that she did not even stop to question why they were wearing sunglasses

in the middle of the night.

'We're here to collect Margaret,' Clementine told her. 'It's very urgent indeed.'

'But nobody has told me anything about this,' complained the nurse. 'And where are you even taking her, anyway?'

'To Professor Jeremiah's clinic,' explained Albert. 'He is going to perform the world's first appendix transplant!'

As Albert said this, Blessing noticed a small puff of steam emerge from the place where his ears would have been. Fortunately, the nurse had other things on her mind.

'But why does Margaret need a new appendix?' asked the nurse.

'Well, of course Professor Jeremiah is not giving her an appendix,' said Albert. 'That would be far too dangerous. No, he is removing an extra one from her!'

'I don't think I understand,' said the nurse.

'Were you born in the summer?' asked Albert.

'Excuse me?' said the nurse.

'When Blessing here was born,' Clementine explained, 'Margaret forgot to give her an appendix. So Margaret has been left with two appendixes inside her – which, of course, is very dangerous, and explains why she has been so sad recently – and meantime this poor little mite has none!'

Blessing tried to look as pitiful and appendix-less as she possibly could.

'That does all sound very serious,' said the nurse, 'but I still don't think I can just let you take Margaret.'

'Entirely up to you,' said Albert. 'But he'll be here any minute, and then you'll have to explain yourself to him.'

'What? Who will be here any minute?' asked the nurse.

'Professor Jeremiah!' said Albert loudly.

'You don't want to get on the wrong side of Professor Jeremiah,' whispered Clementine. 'He is a very important snowman.'

'He's a very important what?' asked the nurse.

'A very important doctor,' said Clementine as Jeremiah came around the corner, sucking on his pipe and wearing

his Sherlock Holmes costume. And the thing about a snowman with a pipe in his mouth who is dressed in a Sherlock Holmes costume is that he does look quite a lot like a very important doctor. Especially if you don't know that his clothes are a costume and his pipe is made of plastic.

'Now then,' boomed Jeremiah, 'what seems to be the hold-up here?'

'There's no hold-up, Professor Jeremiah,' said the nurse quickly. 'I'll fetch your patient right now.'

As soon as the nurse had gone, Blessing turned to Albert. 'An appendix transplant?' she asked him.

'Yes!' said Albert, 'I just invented that operation right then on the spot! I really should have been a Snow Doctor. I would have been excellent at it.'

'You would have been,' agreed Clementine. 'But I think you are perfect just the way you are.'

'Thank you,' said Albert.

'Why have your cheeks turned blue, Albert?' asked Blessing.

'They haven't,' he replied. 'You must be seeing things.'

'Turning blue is how we snowmen blush,' explained Clementine. 'I think I embarrassed Albert by telling him he is perfect just the way he is.'

'Well, I'm not blushing,' said Albert, 'so I have no idea what either of you are talking about. Ahem.'

'Now they've gone purple,' said Blessing.

'I don't know why that has happened,' said Clementine.

'It must be because Albert turns red when he fibs, and red and blue together make purple,' said Blessing.

'How clever!' said Clementine.

'Yes, it is very clever, except I didn't fib, because I wasn't blushing, so there is no reason I'd be turning red or blue, let alone purple,' said Albert, turning a deeper shade of purple even as he spoke.

'It's okay, Albert,' said Clementine. 'I love you just the way you are, fibs and all.'

'And I love you just the way you are,' replied Albert, 'fibs and all too.'

'But I don't ever fib,' said Clementine.

'Yes, and that complete lack of fibbing is one of the reasons I love you,' explained Albert.

Albert and Clementine then gazed dreamily at each other for so long it was as if they thought they were the only ones in the room, or even the whole world.

'Get an igloo already, you two,' muttered Jeremiah, quietly enough that only Blessing and Nelson heard him.

When the nurse returned, she was pushing Margaret in a wheelchair.

'Blessing?' her mum asked. 'Why are you here in the middle of the night? What is going on?'

'I already explained it all to you, Margaret,' said the nurse. 'Professor Jeremiah here is going to perform the world's first appendix transplant on you and your daughter. He's a very important doctor, so there really is nothing to worry about.'

Before Margaret could ask any more questions, Clementine took the wheelchair from the nurse and quickly began wheeling her away. The others hurried after them.

'When will you be bringing Margaret back?' the nurse shouted as they left the ward.

'Before morning,' Jeremiah called back cheerily, 'if everybody survives!'

Outside, Albert and Clementine loaded Margaret into the back of the ambulance.

'Why is there a dog in here?' she asked.

'Don't worry about him,' said Albert. 'He is quite harmless, even though he's a dog.'

Margaret turned to Blessing. 'What is happening?' she asked. 'And where are we going? What is this operation we are having?'

'We're not really having an operation, Mum,' said

Blessing. 'We're actually going to a party. It's a kind of belated birthday party.'

'Whose birthday was it?' Margaret asked.

'It was yours, Mum,' said Blessing.

'Oh. It was just my birthday, wasn't it?' said Margaret. 'And I was so unwell I did not even notice. That is the strangest thing.'

'That's not actually the strangest thing, Mum,' Blessing said. 'Because a stranger thing is that my friends here – well, they're all snowmen.'

The three snowmen now removed their sunglasses and smiled as reassuringly as they could, which, of course, was not very reassuringly at all.

'That's Albert, and that's Clementine, and that is Jeremiah,' said Blessing.

'You can remember me because I am the only one with a pipe,' explained Jeremiah.

'I think I am having the strangest dream,' said Margaret.

'It's not a dream, Mum.'

'But if this is not a dream—' Margaret began and then stopped. Because if it was not a dream then what on earth was it?

'It can be a dream if you want it to be,' said Clementine gently. 'After all, it's the middle of the night and you're being driven to a party in an ambulance with your daughter, three snowmen and a dog. So it does sound like a dream. And, of course, if it really is a dream, then you might as well just lie back and enjoy the ride.'

'Yes,' said Margaret, the faintest hint of a smile beginning to spread across her lips. 'I indeed might as well just lie back and enjoy the ride.'

The ambulance drove past all the late-night things of the city.

The traffic lights.

The bars.

The chicken shops.

The police cars.

The foxes.

Each time they passed a fox, Jeremiah honked the horn, and the fox howled back in delight. Even though foxes are a kind of dog, they are extremely fond of snowmen, and snowmen are equally fond of them. It is just another strange thing in a city that is quite full of them, if you only know where to look.

Twenty-two

Eventually, the ambulance stopped. Clementine and Albert came around and opened the back doors and helped Margaret into her wheelchair. Blessing was the last one to get out, and it took her a moment to realise where they were.

There were no cheery humans working outside tonight. Instead, two large, solemn-looking men blocked the entrance. They wore long coats and dark glasses and

scarves, and if you did not know any better you might think they were gangsters.

'Are you sure the party we are going to is in there?' Margaret asked.

But the men at the door now took off their dark glasses and scarves to reveal that they were also snowmen.

'Welcome, snow friends!' they said. 'Welcome, and Happy Spring Time!'

And then they threw the wide door open, and Blessing wheeled her mum into the Flower Market.

Margaret stared at it all.

At the hundreds of snowmen celebrating.

At the thousands of beautiful flowers.

At the glacier band playing 'Here Comes the Sun'.

And then, quite understandably, Margaret fainted.

The snowmen made a space for Margaret and hurried to bring her ice, because snowmen only ever faint from being too warm. When Margaret came round, the glacier band celebrated her recovery by striking up the St Bernard's Waltz.

Despite being named after a dog, the St Bernard's Waltz is the most beloved dance of all snowmen, and every snowman in the entire Flower Market rushed on to the dance floor. It was quite a sight, and it made Margaret turn to Blessing and smile.

'This is the most wonderful dream,' she said. 'And I think it must mean spring is coming, and I'm going to start feeling better soon.'

'Yes,' said Blessing. 'I think that's what it must mean too.'

The party would go on until dawn, and perhaps even later still. Article Nine of the Snowman Code said all snowmen

could stay out as late as they wanted tonight, whether they had a disguise or not. After all, even if some early morning postwoman did spot a snowman making his way home, nobody would believe her. And, by evening, the snowmen would have all disappeared for another year, anyway.

Still, somebody might have noticed a missing patient, so they drove Margaret back to the hospital before dawn broke. Professor Jeremiah told the nurse that he had successfully performed the world's first appendix transplant, and that the doctors should be on the lookout for a remarkable improvement in Margaret's condition. That made Margaret and Blessing smile at each other, which in turn drew a gasp from the nurse.

'I haven't ever seen you smile like that, Margaret,' she said, before quickly turning to Professor Jeremiah and asking if he might consider performing appendix transplants on all her other patients too.

From the hospital, Jeremiah drove them to Miriam and John's house. They all got out of the ambulance, and Blessing began to tell Albert and Clementine about her brilliant plan for how they could stay in contact with each other. They just had to send Blessing postcards, and she could reunite them every winter, and maybe—

'Ahem,' said Albert. 'Ahem.'

Blessing saw that Albert had turned red.

'What?' she asked. 'What is it now?'

'Blessing, do you remember I once told you how snowmen only have nine lives?' Albert asked.

'No,' said Blessing. 'Because you didn't tell me that. You told me that snowmen go from place to place forever. You said they only say it's nine because that's as high a number as anybody can reasonably be expected to count to.'

'Right, right,' said Albert. 'Well, the thing is, we did always use to go from place to place forever. That is true. But now that the weather is so broken, there is a lot less

snow in the world than there used to be. And unfortunately that means children don't get to build nearly as many snowmen.'

'And what does that mean?' asked Blessing, even though she had a terrible feeling she already knew.

'It means,' said Albert, 'that it is now only the younger snowmen who wake up somewhere new each time they melt. Jeremiah here is just one hundred and fifty winters – a snow baby, really – so after we all melt tomorrow, he will be off on a new adventure in some new winter. But Clementine and I are both older snowmen now and, deep down in our most frozen places, we know this was our last winter.'

Blessing stared at Albert in horror.

'What?' she said. 'No! You've only just found each other after six hundred winters! You can't just melt forever and never see each other again!'

Blessing was too upset to care about even snowmen seeing her cry.

And she did not merely cry, but let out huge, convulsing sobs.

They rumbled up from deep inside and shook her entire body.

They sucked the air from her lungs until she felt like she could not breathe.

They left her gasping.

But then, through all her gasping and her sobbing and her tears, Blessing saw something very strange.

Albert and Clementine were smiling.

'How can you possibly smile,' Blessing eventually managed to get out, 'when you're going to melt and never see each other again?'

'We're smiling because we're going to be together forever now,' said Albert.

'What?' asked Blessing. 'What does that mean?'

'It means,' explained Clementine, 'that even deep down, in our most frozen places, we snowmen are just water. And, after we melt, Albert and I will go back to being water.

And, from then on, the two of us will always be together.'

'You see, the incredible thing about water,' said Albert, 'is that it's all exactly the same stuff. All of it! Every last drop is identical. So, after Clementine and I melt, we will be completely inseparable forever.'

Blessing looked from Albert to Clementine and back again. They seemed to be genuinely happy that they would melt and be forever together, but they were forgetting one important thing.

'But even if you two will always be together,' Blessing said, 'what about me?'

'What about you?' asked Albert.

'I'll miss you,' said Blessing quietly.

'Oh, icebergs!' said Albert. 'Did we forget to tell you that bit? That's just about the most important part: we'll both still always be right here with you too!'

'But how?' asked Blessing. 'How will you still be with me after you've melted?'

'It's really quite simple,' explained Albert. 'If all water

is exactly the same, then wherever you see water, that will be us. So, if you see the rain running down your classroom window on a Thursday afternoon in autumn, that will be us. Or we might be the leaky tap dripping in your bathroom, or the cool ice in your drink on a summer day. We'll be right there with you in your tears any time you cry, of course. And, if you ever manage to visit Africa, we'll be all the snow at the South Pole.'

'The South Pole is in Antarctica,' said Blessing, throwing her arms around Albert Framlington and burying her head deep in his snowy chest.

They stayed like that for a very long time, and then a bathroom light went on in Miriam and John's house and Nelson started yelping that he had been very patient with all this snowman business, but they really must go inside now.

'I'm not ready to say goodbye just yet,' Blessing said. 'I'll come and see you in the park tomorrow morning before—'

She let the sentence trail off.

'We'd like that,' said Albert. 'But only if you have time.'

'Of course I have time,' said Blessing.

'Blessing, before you go inside,' said Jeremiah, 'I was wondering if, well – that thing you said about postcards. I was thinking that, maybe after I melt, perhaps you could look out for my pipe? And then next winter I could send you a postcard to tell you where I am, and maybe you could send the pipe back to me. I wouldn't normally ask, but it is rather a special pipe.'

'Of course I can do that for you, Jeremiah,' said Blessing.

'You and your pipe,' sighed Albert.

Twenty-three

Blessing and Nelson went inside and crept upstairs.

But even though dawn was already breaking outside, they did not go straight to bed. Instead, Blessing tiptoed along the hallway to Miriam and John's art cupboard, and Nelson paw-padded after her. Blessing quietly searched through the supplies until she found what she needed, and then the two of them crept back to their room. There, Blessing closed the door and swiftly but silently made the

most important art project she ever would.

Only after she had finished the art project did they actually go to bed. Nelson immediately fell fast asleep and started quietly snoring. But though she had stayed up all night – and even made an art project too – Blessing could not sleep.

At first, she thought it must just be because of all the excitement of the party. But it had already been hours since they had left the party.

And then she wondered if maybe Nelson's snoring was keeping her awake, but everybody knows that listening to the sound of a dog quietly snoring is a more reliable method of falling asleep than even counting sheep.

Then, as she lay awake, Blessing suddenly had another idea good enough to make her whisper, 'Yes!' She therefore decided that the idea must have been the reason she couldn't sleep. After all, her brain had to have been working overtime to come up with an idea as good as that. Yet, even after she'd had her good idea, Blessing still could not sleep.

So Blessing then decided what had actually been keeping her awake all this time was the dawn light coming through the gap in the curtains. A little later, she realised it was no longer even dawn light, but actual daylight, and so of course that must be what was keeping her awake.

But just a little later still, Blessing realised that it had not been all the excitement, nor Nelson's quiet snoring, nor the good idea, nor the dawn light, nor even the daylight that had been keeping her awake all this time. No, what had been keeping her awake was the fact that she was too warm. But if Blessing felt too warm, that meant—

Blessing jumped out of bed, threw her dressing gown over her pyjamas, grabbed her art project, ran downstairs and hurried out the back door.

Nelson did the same, except he did not throw his dressing gown over his pyjamas, because dogs do not generally wear dressing gowns or even pyjamas. He also did not grab his art project, because dogs only rarely do art projects.

Outside, there was no sun yet and the sky was still filled with dark winter clouds. But the air already felt much warmer than it had last night, and the snow in Miriam and John's back garden had begun to melt. When Blessing reached the street, she saw something even worse: the snow on the road had already almost completely melted.

Thud-thud-thud-thud.

Pitter-patter-pitter-patter.

Blessing and Nelson raced through the streets towards the park. The front gardens they passed all still had snow in them, but here too the roads were almost completely clear. When they reached the entrance to the park, Blessing helped Nelson squeeze through the bars of the gate. She then quickly climbed to the top, jumped down and—

Crunch-splat!

Blessing fell in a heap.

For months, every time she had jumped from the top of the gate, she had landed in deep snow. Now there was not even enough snow left to properly cushion her fall.

Blessing dusted herself off and hurried on into the park. Nelson shook himself off in sympathy and chased after her. The snow on the road through the park had melted too, so Blessing ran ever faster, and Nelson did the same.

As she crossed the bridge over the duck pond, Blessing saw that the water below was no longer frozen. The ducks quacked at her to tell her it was still too cold for swimming, but that is ducks for you, always complaining.

Thud-thud-thud-thud.

Pitter-patter-pitter-patter.

Glancing upwards as she ran, Blessing saw the sun was still nowhere to be seen and the sky remained full of winter clouds. But she could feel that the air here in the park was warmer even than it had been in Miriam and John's street.

And if the snow in Miriam and John's garden had already started to melt—

And the snow on the roads had almost already gone—

And the snow beneath the park gate had been so much thinner—

And the ice on the duck pond had all disappeared, then—

When she reached the pitches, Blessing stopped dead and stared at what lay ahead of her.

And breathed a deep sigh of relief.

The pitches were still blanketed in snow, and at the far end of them stood two familiar snowmen.

Crunch-slurp-crunch-slurp.

Blessing ran as fast as she could over the pitches towards Albert and Clementine.

Crunch-crunch-crunch-crunch.

And so too did Nelson, which is really quite something when you stop and think about it.

'Albert!' Blessing called out as she ran. 'Clementine!'

Neither snowman turned around to look at her.

'Please don't melt yet!' shouted Blessing. 'I'm coming!'

But, as Blessing neared them, she realised that both Albert and Clementine were already a little smaller than they used to be. And, when she reached them, she saw

that one of Albert's bottle-top eyes had slipped lower than the other, and Clementine's button nose had fallen off entirely.

'Albert?' Blessing said.

But Albert did not respond.

'Clementine?' Blessing asked, her voice now slightly cracking.

Clementine did not respond either.

Her friends were gone.

Blessing gently fixed Albert's bottle-tops and replaced Clementine's button. Then, from out of her dressing-gown pocket, she took the art project she had made at dawn: a pair of home-made gold medals. They weren't made of real gold, of course, just gold foil paper wrapped round a circle of cardboard. But Blessing was known for her skill at cutting circles and John always bought the good gold foil, so they looked very real, and maybe even more real than some actual gold medals do. Best of all, each of them dangled from a thick length of bright red ribbon that Blessing now

used to hang them around Albert and Clementine's necks.

'I'm sorry I got here too late,' she told them. 'I really wanted to say goodbye to you both. And Albert, I wanted to tell you that you were my best friend. You saved me from the Driplet Triplets. And maybe you didn't always follow the Snowman Code, but I know you always wanted to, and that's exactly the same thing, isn't it? And you both chose to melt so that my mum would get better, even though you knew this was your very last winter. That's the kindest thing anyone has ever done for us. It's the kindest thing I've ever even heard of, and you both deserve real gold medals for it. And I know it can't help either of you now, but last night I had another good idea. I've decided that, when I grow up, I'm going to become a scientist and help to fix this broken weather, so in the future no more snowmen will have to melt forever.'

Just after she said that, Blessing imagined she saw a small puff of steam emerge from the place where Albert's ears would have been. It was as if Albert had heard

Blessing's brilliant idea, and believed he had thought of it entirely by himself.

But Blessing knew that could not possibly have happened.

Because Albert Framlington was gone.

But then Blessing noticed one corner of Albert's mouth move ever so slightly upwards. At first, she assumed he must just be melting. But melting things go downwards, not upwards. And then she saw the opposite corner of Albert's mouth move slightly upwards too.

'Albert!' Blessing said. 'Albert? Albert? Albert? Albert? Albert?'

As soon as Blessing had spoken his name for the sixth time, Albert turned to her and arranged his features into a wide grin. Blessing let out a sound that was somewhere between a relieved sob and the kind of noise you should really count to ten before making.

'Albert!' she said. 'Why did you pretend you couldn't hear me? I thought I'd missed you!'

'Because of the Snowman Code, of course!' said Albert.

'Albert wanted to make sure you remembered it for next winter,' added Clementine.

'Of course I'll remember it,' said Blessing. 'I'll never forget it.'

'Is that an ice promise?' asked Albert.

'Yes,' said Blessing, 'it is.'

'Good,' said Albert. 'Because ice promises are unbreakable.'

'I know they are,' said Blessing. 'That's why I had to bring you a gold medal, remember?'

'Right!' said Albert. 'And thank you, because I really do love my medal. It makes me feel very proud to have been awarded it.'

'Me too,' agreed Clementine. 'And just look how precious they are!'

'They're not actually real gold,' explained Blessing. 'I made them.'

'And that's exactly what makes them so precious!' said

Clementine. 'All the most precious things are made by children.'

'Yes, like snowmen, for instance,' said Albert.

'That wasn't exactly what I had in mind,' said Clementine.

Albert did not seem to hear this, or perhaps chose not to.

'By the way, Blessing,' he said, 'you forgot to mention all the facts I taught you.'

'What facts?' asked Blessing. 'What are you talking about?'

'When you were saying all those nice things about me,' said Albert. 'You forgot to mention that I also taught you many interesting facts.'

'None of them were true,' said Blessing.

'Icicles!' said Albert. 'For instance, I taught you that Sherlock Holmes was a famous zookeeper, and that an encyclopedia is a sort of dictionary of animals, and that the phrase "better later than never"—'

But something in the distance seemed to catch Albert's attention then, and he let the sentence trail off as he turned to stare at it.

Blessing followed Albert's gaze, but there was nothing at all there to see.

Nothing except the snowy pitches.

And the Rose Garden.

And beyond them all the tall buildings of the city.

And up above it all, shining down on the whole city, the sun.

The sun!

Nobody had seen it in months.

And it had only just broken through the clouds.

But it was already warming the pitches so quickly that in some places steam had now begun to rise from the ground.

In fact, Blessing could even feel its warmth on her face.

And so she looked across to Albert.

The sunlight had caught his bottle-tops and it was making them sparkle in a way Blessing had never seen before. Clementine was staring in the same direction as Albert, and her mismatched marbles were sparkling in exactly the same way. Hearing a rustling noise, Blessing looked down and saw that Albert had taken Clementine's snowy hand in his.

'Albert?' asked Blessing quietly. 'Is this—'

'It's nothing to worry about,' said Albert. 'Nothing to worry about at all. I just wish you could see it, Blessing. It's all so beautiful.'

'See what?' asked Blessing. 'What's all so beautiful?'

'The water,' said Albert. 'There's so much water. And oh, the flowers!'

'Geraniums,' agreed Clementine. 'And carnations.'

'Chrysanthemums too,' said Albert. 'So many beautiful chrysanthemums.'

'We're such lucky snowmen,' said Clementine.

'Yes, we really are,' agreed Albert.

And, with those words, the two snowmen fell silent.

And then, even as Blessing watched, the sparkling in her friends' bottle-tops and mismatched marbles gently dimmed until it was merely a twinkling, and then nothing more than an ordinary reflection.

'Albert?' Blessing whispered. 'Clementine?'

Neither snowman answered, and deep in her most frozen places Blessing knew that even if she said their names another hundred times they would not reply. This time, they really had gone.

Sure enough, a few moments later, Blessing heard a quiet cracking.

And then Albert Framlington fell to his lopside.

This caused him to lean heavily on Clementine.

And Albert leaning on her caused Clementine to fall in on herself.

And Clementine falling in on herself sent Albert tumbling to the ground.

And then, a moment later, Blessing herself fell into the snow amongst them.

Just as if her very own heart had melted too.

Twenty-four

Being a very good boy, Nelson knew exactly what to do.

He ran home and barked so loudly at Miriam and John that they understood to follow him, even though they did not speak a single word of Dog. Nelson then led them straight to the park, to where Blessing lay amid two unremarkable-looking piles of melting snow. But Miriam and John could not wake her up, and so John picked her up and carried her home. When they got there, they tucked

Blessing up in bed and called for Dr Kumar to come as quickly as he could.

When Dr Kumar arrived, he was wearing his most serious expression.

He took Blessing's temperature with a thermometer.

He listened to her chest with his stethoscope.

He took her blood pressure with the thing doctors use to measure blood pressure.

He even lifted each of Blessing's eyelids and shone a little torch in.

But through it all Blessing did not stir.

And so finally Dr Kumar took a feather from his bag and carefully tickled all her toes.

When even this did not rouse her, Dr Kumar turned to Miriam and John and solemnly told them his diagnosis: Blessing was completely and utterly fast asleep.

She must not be disturbed under any circumstances.

Twenty-five

When Blessing finally awoke, the clock told her it was six in the evening.

Nelson was sitting on the end of the bed. He looked at her and tilted his head to the right. Blessing understood enough Dog to know this meant there was important news. And so she rushed downstairs, where she found Miriam and John in the kitchen.

'You're awake!' said John. 'How are you feeling?'

'I'm fine,' said Blessing. 'But has something happened? Is there news?'

'There is news, actually,' said Miriam. 'It's to do with your mum.'

Blessing felt her stomach tie itself in an unexpected knot. Perhaps it had not been such a good idea to kidnap Margaret and tell the nurse they were taking her for an appendix transplant after all. What if that doctor who wanted everyone to be disappointed as soon as possible tried to give Margaret another appendix to replace the one she thought Professor Jeremiah had removed?

'No need to look so worried!' said Miriam. 'It's good news.'

'Yes!' added John. 'Your mum's feeling much better.'

'Then can we go and visit her at the hospital tonight?' asked Blessing.

'Oh no,' said Miriam. 'I'm afraid that is completely out of the question.'

'But if she's feeling better—' began Blessing.

'The reason we can't visit her at the hospital,' interrupted John, 'is because she has already been discharged!'

'And Jasmine says you can go home whenever you're ready,' added Miriam.

No wonder Nelson had tilted his head to the right. This was such important news that it left Blessing speechless for only the third time in her ten-and-a-half winters and summers.

'But how could my mum get so much better in a single day?' she eventually asked.

And that was when Blessing discovered she had been asleep for three whole days and two entire nights.

Perhaps it had been the shock of seeing her good friends melt.

Or maybe it had been because there were no snowmen to bring her ice to revive her.

Or perhaps, after so many night-time adventures with

the world's only nocturnal marsupials, Blessing simply had a lot of sleep to catch up on.

None of us will ever know.

Not even Dr Kumar could tell you.

Twenty-six

When Blessing got outside, it seemed just like any other evening in late May.

There was no snow anywhere.

The sun was shining in a cloudless blue sky.

And nobody she passed on the street was even talking about the weather now.

Instead, they were talking about barbecues and summer holidays and trips to the seaside.

The park gates were open, so Blessing did not even need to climb over them. The ducks still quacked at her as she crossed the bridge, but this time it was only to complain that somebody had brought them the wrong kind of bread earlier. And then Blessing turned the corner and saw the pitches.

She had almost forgotten they could even look like that.

There was so much green grass, covered in so many kids.

They were playing tig, and football, and flying kites.

Some of them were just plain old-fashioned rough-and-tumbling each other.

And of course there were a great number of dogs chasing tennis balls.

And plenty of old people doing their tai chi.

Blessing made her way across the pitches and stopped somewhere near the middle. On the ground beneath her lay two bottle-tops, a small old potato, two twigs and a scarf. Next to them were a pair of marbles, a button and

a slightly crooked stick. Blessing bent down, carefully gathered all the objects up and continued on her way. The gold medals on red ribbons had been nowhere to be seen, so perhaps a pair of passing magpies had awarded them to themselves.

As Blessing neared the Rose Garden, the air suddenly grew heavy with a smell she had not realised how much she had missed. Sure enough, when she passed under the stone archway, she saw the roses had already bloomed.

Yellow roses and red roses.

Pink roses and white roses.

Purple roses and lilac roses.

Roses that were too many different colours all at once to even name.

There were so many good-looking rose bushes that it took Blessing some time to find the prettiest and sweetest-smelling of them all. She carefully buried her friends' decorations beneath it, then stood back and solemnly told them that she would never forget her ice promise.

As she turned to leave the Rose Garden, Blessing noticed a girl of about her own age crouched behind the stone archway. She must have been there the whole time because she smiled at Blessing, then whispered, 'What's an ice promise?'

'It's a promise you have to always keep,' Blessing whispered back. 'I learned that from my snowman friends.'

The girl smiled at her in the polite way people do when they are sure they must have misheard you.

'What are you doing down there, anyway?' asked Blessing.

'Hide-and-seek,' replied the girl. 'You can hide with me if you like?'

'Thanks,' Blessing whispered. 'But maybe tomorrow.'

As Blessing walked out of the Rose Garden and back into the park, her heart suddenly felt heavy in her chest.

It was true that she did not have to worry about the

Driplet Triplets any more.

And she could go to school like every other kid.

And the endless winter was over.

And her mum was out of hospital.

And everything really was going to be okay now.

But still.

That thing Albert and Clementine had told her about always being there for her? It had sounded really nice when they said it. But, well, it just wasn't actually true, was it? How could it possibly be true when Blessing had watched them both melt?

No, her friends were gone forever.

But right then, in the middle of Victoria Park, on the third night of the latest spring London had ever known, something magical happened.

It started with an underground rumbling sound so deep that Blessing thought it must be an earthquake. There were not supposed to be earthquakes in London. But then there was not supposed to be an Abominable Snowman

in Victoria Park either. And the rumbling sound beneath her kept getting louder and louder, so what else could it possibly be?

The other kids all heard it too, and stopped playing football and tig and rough-and-tumbling each other.

And the dogs heard it and stopped chasing their tennis balls.

Even the old people heard it and stopped doing their tai chi, and old people are every bit as bad at hearing as snowmen.

And just when Blessing was trying to remember what you are supposed to do in an earthquake—

The rumbling stopped.

And for a brief moment Victoria Park fell completely silent.

Kids and dogs and old people exchanged puzzled glances.

Perhaps the rumbling had just been one of those things after all.

And it was time to get back on with their football and

tig and rough-and-tumble and tennis balls and tai chi.

But before any kid, dog or old person could do any of that—

Every single sprinkler on the Victoria Park pitches suddenly hissed into life!

And the kids all screamed and ran to wherever they could find a dry place.

And the dogs all followed them and so – eventually – did the old people.

But not Blessing.

Blessing did the exact opposite.

She walked right out into the middle of the pitches to where the sprays from half a dozen sprinklers now met each other in the place where Albert Framlington had once stood.

And she stood right in the middle of them all, letting the water soak her completely through.

Looking at the tiny rainbows the evening sunlight made as it passed through the spray.

And knowing that what silly old Albert Framlington had said had been true all along.

Her snow friends would always be with her now.

Twenty-seven

If you had been at the West Entrance of Victoria Park that summer evening, you might have seen a ten-and-a-half-year-old girl bend down and pick something out of the grass on her way out.

But you would not have seen much more than that.

Because as soon as Blessing reached the park gates, she started to run.

And not long after that she was running down her street.

And into her house.

And into the kitchen.

And right into her mum's arms.

Later that night—

After Margaret had asked Blessing why she was soaked through.

And then insisted Blessing have a nice warm shower.

After Blessing had pointed out it did not make very much sense that the solution to getting soaked with all her clothes on was to get soaked with all her clothes off.

After they had eaten home-made pizza that had tomato sauce and was therefore truly home-made pizza and not merely cheese on toast.

After they had played endless rounds of the A to Z of London game.

After they had done all that, and as Margaret tucked Blessing into her own bed—

She picked up a small plastic object from Blessing's bedside table.

'Blessing,' she asked, 'is this a pipe?'

'It's just a pretend one,' said Blessing. 'It's for a snowman.'

'A snowman?' said Margaret. 'When I was in the hospital, I had such a strange dream about snowmen. You were in it too. You told me that snowmen are all alive and if you speak to them seven times they must answer you.'

'It's six times!' said Blessing.

'Then next winter we will have to build a snowman, and make sure to talk to him six times. Who knows, maybe he will even answer us!' said Margaret.

'He'll have to answer us,' said Blessing, 'because it's the Snowman Code.'

Margaret only laughed, and Blessing decided not to say any more.

What was the point?

Her mum thought it had all been a dream and she would not believe Blessing.

At least not until next winter.

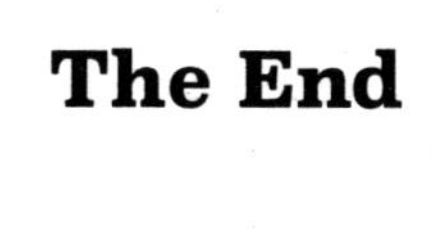

A NOTE FOR READERS OF ALL AGES

Thank you for reading *The Snowman Code*. I hope you enjoyed hearing the story of Blessing and Albert and their friends as much as I enjoyed sharing it with you. I did my best to set it down just exactly as I first heard it all those years ago, so hopefully I did not miss out anything too important. If I got anything wrong, I am sure I will hear about it from Blessing soon enough.

For Albert's part, now that you have reached the end of his story, I think he would have simply wanted to remind you about the many other wonderful books available to read at your local safari park. He'd have whispered to you that even books containing no snowmen and hardly any flowers can be surprisingly good, and a safari park near you undoubtedly has more than nine such books waiting for you to read them. He'd then have added that exactly the same thing went for aquariums too.

Blessing would have rolled her eyes then and told you that Albert did not mean safari parks and aquariums, he meant libraries and bookshops. Albert would have thought about this and then shaken his snowy head and said no, he definitely meant safari parks and aquariums and perhaps Blessing ought to try looking them up in the atlas if she did not know what they were.

The one thing I know they would both agree on is that if you ever find yourself standing outside on a day when the ground beneath your feet suddenly freezes, and you look up to the sky and see snowflakes falling from dark clouds, well, the very best thing you can do on a day like that is to build yourself a snowman.

And if you find that you can't build a snowman because it turns out the snow is actually falling inside, well, then you can always draw yourself a picture of a snowman, or write yourself a story about one, or perhaps even just think about one. They will be glad to meet you, for they have been my friends for a long time and now they will always be yours too. The most important thing is to make sure you introduce yourself to your new snowman friend six times. That, after all, is only polite.